KELLY'S BAR

KELLY'S BAR

JOE MONTE

Columbus, Ohio

Kelly's Bar

Published by Gatekeeper Press
2167 Stringtown Rd, Suite 109
Columbus, OH 43123-2989
www.GatekeeperPress.com

The cover was designed by Kevin Akers @ www.kevinakers.com.

ISBN (paperback): 9781642377255
eISBN: 9781642377262

NOTE FROM THE AUTHOR

I was born in San Francisco and moved to Sunnyvale in 1973. Sunnyvale is the center of Silicon Valley and home to high-tech workers new to the area. Google, Linked-In, Facebook and Apple have erased our agricultural roots. We have a rich history that most are unaware of. For example, Sunnyvale was home to The Joshua Hendy Iron Works, founded in San Francisco in the 1850s, which moved to Sunnyvale after the Great San Francisco earthquake of 1906. They manufactured mining equipment and built hundreds of engines for the Navy's fleet of Victory Ships in both World War I and II.

My background is in finance and I never excelled in writing. However, I think I have a great imagination. In 2000, I sustained a serious back injury which required surgery. I had an idea for a story and started writing it down. This helped distract me from my pain. Soon, I became engrossed in this wild plot centered around a bartender. But once I recovered, I needed to get back to work.

In 2017, surgery was again required to repair another back injury. Are you seeing a pattern here? I soon picked up the novel where I had left off. Now I was hooked. Eventually, I finished my first novel. My novel truly has a back story.

In *Kelly's Bar*, I introduce the reader to our roots and history wrapped around the story of Bill, an unscrupulous bartender. Bill takes a laptop computer from a customer who meets an untimely end in the bar. Mary, his wife, finds a fantastic novel hidden on the computer. Bill opens a can of worms when he decides to have it published with him as the author, resulting in Mary's arrest for espionage.

The reader discovers Sunnyvale starting in 1933 through Bill's uncle, John Kelly, who built the bar to coincide with the end of Prohibition. John witnesses the last lynching in California. More history o the Bay Area is revealed through Bill's family and Bill growing up.

I hope you enjoy reading this book as
much as I enjoyed writing it.

I want to thank, first my wife Vickie who has put up with me for 45 years. Next I became a much better writer with the support of The Odd Writer's League. Special thanks to all the members especially Jessica, Sinead, Rachael, Abhirup, Alix Liz, Venessa, and the entire group.

My Brother Dan and his wife Bonnie gave me great encouragement and read the early drafts.

My Children, Ellie who also gave me encouragement and Matthew who was the object of most the pranks I used in the book,

—Joe Monte

CHAPTER 1

September 14, 2000. 9:00 a.m.

Clouds darkened the morning light. Mary was silent, staring straight ahead and chewing on her thumbnail as Bill circled the block. He found a parking space on North First Street and struggled, zig-zagging back and forth four times to wedge his red El Camino into the tight space, saying "Fuck" every time he needed to switch directions. They were just two blocks from Darleen Lynch's office, one block from the county courthouse. The street was lined with a mix of modern and 1940s-era office buildings. The sidewalk was already crowded with office workers, attorneys and plaintiffs off to court. The makeshift campsites lining the street smelled of urine; bodies covered by blankets lay next to shopping carts filled with rumpled, black garbage bags. The homeless crawled wearily out of their encampments to avoid the daily police sweep meant to clean up the downtown.

Bill walked around to the front of the car and opened the door for Mary. His gelled black hair was combed straight back, his paisley dress shirt tucked under blue jeans emblazoned with an oversized "Anchor Steam Beer" belt buckle. Mary abruptly pushed him away and stepped out, her black skirt clinging to her petite frame. Her right arm quivered and Bill could see she that was on the verge of an anxiety attack.

"Don't worry," he said without turning to see her face. "You didn't do anything wrong. They can't prove anything."

She turned her face away from him. She had chest pains. Her right arm spasmed, flying over her head as she stuttered, "Don't talk to me!" Perspiration stained the underarms of her white lace blouse and her bright red curls were matted with sweat. "Youu... ass... hole. I told you... couldn't get away with this." She marched down the street without waiting while Bill locked the truck.

"Wait up!" Bill called as he jogged a full block to catch up to her. "We're early. Let's get a cup of coffee." He reached for Mary's hand but she ignored him. For the first time, Bill didn't feel in control of the situation. "You're having an anxiety attack and it's all my fault. I know I screwed up but we need to talk before we see the attorneys."

Mary turned around to face Bill. She was shaking and stuttering. Tears rolled down her cheeks. "I begged you not to do this." She was unable to continue, turning away to walk quickly down First Street.

Bill was one step behind her. "Please stop so we can talk! I know I should have listened to you... I just got carried away. There's a coffee shop right here; we have a half hour to kill." He rushed ahead and opened the door, hoping Mary would follow. She stopped and looked at Bill holding the door.

"Fucker." She turned and started to enter the building and spotted four men in suits running toward the building. "Bill, look." She pointed behind them.

Quickly the men slammed the door closed before Mary could enter.

Tony Polanski was in charge and looked like it. His broad gym-pumped shoulders stretched his suit jacket. He had pale blue eyes and a blond flat-top haircut. He pulled out his FBI badge and an envelope. "Mary Giovanni?"

Two of the other men held Bill back. "You can't do this!" Bill shouted. As he began to struggle against their grasp, one agent shoved him to the ground, pressing Bill's face into the pavement.

Polanski and his partner, Jack McFee, spun Mary around and crammed her into the glass door. The metal frame of the door pressed painfully into her face and chest. Tony pulled his handcuffs out but Mary's right arm flung above her head. Jack grabbed her wrist and yanked it down so Tony could cuff her, telling her, "You are under arrest for espionage and releasing classified military information."

Mary struggled, her body flailing from side to side. Jack patted his hands up and down her legs, then felt the front and back of her sweat-soaked blouse check-ing for weapons. The two agents then lifted her like a rag doll and carried her to a black sedan.

Her body in spasms, her suspended legs kicking above the sidewalk, Mary cried, "I, I, didn't!!"

CHAPTER 2

August 13, 2000. 1:00 p.m.
(Four weeks earlier)

It was a warm day and the smell of syrup and pan-cakes lingered as it drifted down Mathilda Avenue. Bill had just left the auto parts store with a new fan belt when he saw Little Pat Riley bending down to pick up a half-smoked cigarette butt in the gutter by Denny's. Pat was less than five feet tall, his body bent and unable to stand straight. A large hump protruded from his upper back. When Bill was thirteen, Pat was a bigger-than-life personality, living the high life, and a regular at the bar owned by Bill's Uncle John. He was a favorite jockey, well known at the Bay Meadows racetrack.

Bill watched the man's hand tremble. "Little Pat, it's been a long time."

Pat straightened up as much as he could while dis-creetly pushing the butt closer to the sidewalk edge with his shoe. He looked confused and only a shell of his former self.

Bill continued, "I'm Bill from Kelly's Bar. How have you been?"

"I'm doin' good. Still at the track, cleaning out fuckin' stables for Thomas Carter." Years before, Little Pat Riley had been one of the best jockeys on the West Coast. He had won a lot of races for Mr. Carter on cheap, second-rate horses.

Bill pulled a pack of Camels from the pocket of his black silk shirt. He put one in his mouth and handed one to Pat. As they smoked, Bill looked at his knock-off Rolex. The fake gold finish was tarnished and showed a hint of green oxidization. He motioned to Denny's door, "I have time for lunch; will you join me?"

Bill ordered a BLT and beer. Pat gobbled down a T-bone steak, eggs, toast, and two beers as if he hadn't eaten for a week. Bill listened to Pat's stories about horses and his tales of being a jockey. "Life was going great until Carter put me on a stallion called The Real Deal. He was the sire of Raise a Native, the best horse of all time. The cheap bastard got this crazy horse from a claiming race. He didn't take well to being ridden. Out of the gate, I pulled the reins hard to try to get him straight, but we slammed into another horse, breaking my kneecap. He bucked me off and another stupid horse tripped over me, breaking my back. It was months before I could even walk again." Bill picked up the tab. "I can pay," Pat said. "You only had a sandwich."

"Don't worry about it; you were a good friend to my Uncle John. I was just a kid but I loved hearing your stories."

"OK. But only if you take a tip on a horse. It's a fix."

"Thanks, Pat."

Pat looked around as if the police were spying on him. He talked in a low, slow, deep voice. "Yesterday, Geno Bruno brought in a new three-year-old, Shady Sis, to Bay Meadows early in the morning where nobody would see her. I have never seen a horse this strong. Her first race is today at Golden Gate Fields, where nobody knows her. I'm going to put a Jackson down on the race."

Bill sat quietly and just listened to Pat. Realizing how lucky he was to have run into him, Bill reached into his wallet and gave Pat forty dollars. "Thanks, add this to your bet."

Later that afternoon, Bill rushed to the bar to take over for Ignacio. Every city has the types of bars you find on Murphy Street: a micro-brewery, very trendy, with music so loud you couldn't carry on a conversation. The drink menu had fancy names given to daiquiris and martinis. The place was always packed and a great place to pick up a date. The sports bar across the street was a good spot to meet up with your friends and catch a couple of innings of the game while you decided where else to go. The Sunnyvale Bar and Grill tried to combine crappy fast food with a place to get a drink. This was a place you could take your family.

Kelly's was just a quiet bar where you went to have a couple of drinks with people you knew. The building was only twenty-five feet wide and had no windows, only a faded plastic sign and a brown wood-plank door. Behind the bar was an intricate, hand-carved walnut case with glass shelves full of whiskey, gins, tequilas, and vodkas. On the wall hung an old weather-worn, cracked cedar sign proclaiming, **KELLY'S BAR** *Beer 5¢ - Martini 21¢*. Kelly's Bar only offered peanuts, alcohol, a single TV above the bar, and the companionship of regulars.

Bill knew what Charlie would want without asking. He reached for a bottle of Jameson and made a whiskey sour. He placed the drink on the bar in front of Charlie, a well-dressed elderly man with deep wrinkles and a large, vein-covered nose. Charlie oscillated the ice cubes around the glass. "I got two grand riding on your nag in the fifth. I hope that fuckin' tip you got comes through."

"It's a sure thing. I bet five hundred," Bill barked back at Charlie.

Charlie stared at Bill. Bill hoped to reassure him: "The tip was from Little Pat Riley."

"You saw Little Pat? I haven't seen him in here since his accident."

Only Charlie and Bill were watching the TV. The horse's names were superimposed above each gate. Shady Sis was on the outside in gate eleven. The trainers and jockeys were positioning the horses into their gates; the whites of the animals' eyes shined and their muscles rippled as they were part tugged and part coaxed into position. José Santos, in a bright green jacket and cap, stood up on the stirrups to help navigate Shady Sis into her gate. The bell sounded, the gates flew open, and eleven horses charged out. Shady Sis bolted, almost throwing the jockey to the ground. José regained control and she raced out of the gate a full length behind the other horses.

Bill yelled, "Fuck!"

Charlie set his whiskey sour down. "Relax, it's eight furlongs."

Shady Sis raced on the outside, quickly catching up. The jockey stood high in the stirrups, slapping Shady Sis's hind quarters with his crop as she accelerated down the mile track. The announcer said, "This is Shady Sis's first race... Look how she is just flying past the pack!"

At the eight pole, Shady Sis was even with the favorite, Gold Digger. José Santos pulled her toward the inside rail, cutting just barely in front of Gold Digger, who had been leading the whole way. Within seconds, Shady Sis pulled ahead of Gold Digger.

Bill and Charlie pounded on the teak wood bar and screamed, "Go Shady, go Shady!"

Tom, Greg, and even Hippie Paul left his computer in the back booth to see what the commotion was about.

At the three-quarter-mile mark, Shady was ahead by four lengths and still pulling away. Bill and Charlie continued screaming, "Go, go, go!" When Shady Sis crossed the finish line, she was six lengths ahead of Gold Digger.

The tote board listed the results and payouts. Shady Sis was at the top with 30 to 1 to win, 10 to 1 to place, and 5 to 1 to show. The track announcer screamed, "Who could see this coming? What a debut!"

Bill high-fived Charlie and yelled, "I just made fifteen grand." He paused for a second in disbelief. "My god, you just made sixty grand," Bill realized, thinking he should had bet more.

Charlie smiled. "Shit, we need to thank Little Pat for that tip." He raised his glass. "Thanks, Bill. I think I can finally tell my boss to shove it!"

"Drinks for everyone!" Bill poured Tom, Greg, and Paul another draft beer and made another drink for Charlie and himself.

The TV switched from Shady Sis in the winner's circle back to the tote board flashing **under review** on the top line next to Shady Sis's name. The announcer said, "Bob, I think they are looking at how close Shady Sis was when she cut in front of Gold Digger at the eight pole. If she interfered at all, they will disqualify her." A close-up in slow motion showed no contact, but Shady Sis's rear hoofs were within inches of Gold Digger's front legs.

"What the fuck?!" Bill angrily downed his drink. "They never touched! This is bullshit."

Bill stared at the TV when the tote board message changed to "Disqualified."

"Shady Sis has been disqualified for interfering with Gold Digger at the eight pole," explained the track announcer.

"What!? They can't do that!" Bill yelled at the TV. "Fuck, fuck!" He looked at Charlie in disbelief. He didn't give Charlie time to comment before he continued. "Shady Sis won; it wasn't even close!" He paced behind the bar, not wanting to hear anything from anybody. "Shit! Shit!"

Charlie downed his drink. "What are you going to do about Lawrence when he comes in tomorrow?"

Bill wasn't ready to deal with this yet, as he thought, Damn I am screwed. Why did I bet so much? "Shit, I don't know what I'm gonna do. Charlie, what are you gonna to do? You owe him two grand."

"Give me another drink." Bill didn't bother making a whisky sour. He just poured them both a large glass of Jameson on the rocks.

"It will kill me but I can pull it out of my 401K," Charlie said.

Bill thought about Lawrence and the fuckin' boss he worked for. That asshole would break my legs for five hundred bucks. "Charlie, I was sure we'd win."

"Shit happens. It just didn't work out. What about you? Will you be OK?"

Bill was sweating. "I have maybe fifty bucks. I don't know what I'll do. I can't borrow any more from Ignacio. Shit, I'm stuck here till two!"

CHAPTER 3

The Next morning:

"This coffee is shit! How can you screw up a pot of coffee?" Bill plopped his mug on the yellow, chipped tile counter, spilling his coffee into the cracked grout. He scooped hash brown potatoes from the cast iron skillet, then opened the refrigerator and stared at the top shelf. "Where the hell are the eggs? I wanted scrambled eggs! Son of a bitch!"

Bill was still in last night's clothes; his shirt smelled of spilled beer and showed stains from spilled drinks. He had hardly slept from worrying about how he would pay Lawrence. Lawrence was a good guy, but he worked for an asshole bookie who never cut anyone a break. Bill remembered Chuck coming into the bar, his face black and blue and a full cast on his right leg. Chuck had been a track star at San Jose State; his career ended. Shit, he would never say what happened, but Bill knew he made bets with Lawrence. Bill remembered when Lawrence finally came into the bar, two weeks later, how upset he was about Chuck.

Bill heard Mary yell from the bathroom, "I'm sorry, dear, but I didn't know we were out of eggs."

"Damn it. I don't know why you can't do a few simple things. Just make sure you have eggs when you get home tonight."

"Co-could you get Johnny ready; he didn't have his shoes and s-socks on last time I checked."

Bill lifted four strips of bacon with a spatula and slapped them down on a paper towel, "Damn it! Do I have to do everything? You just can't let me think. I have a lot to do today. Did you make his damn lunch yet?"

Mary walked into the kitchen holding the hairbrush up like a club. Her out-of-control, Little Orphan Annie red hair covered the oversized collar of her white blouse. "No, I haven't." She paused, trying not to stutter. "Would you mind? I can't be late again."

Bill grabbed the coffee mug, making a face after a short swig of the bitter brew. "OK, but it's like I do everything." He added some bourbon to the coffee.

Mary bit a rough edge off her fingernail and continued to get ready for work.

Bill filled a glass with milk. "Johnny, get your butt out here, and you better be ready for school. I'm going to count to five! ONE... TWO-O... THREE-E...," Bill shouted each number louder, but stretched out the syllables.

"FOUR-R." He paused for three seconds.

"FIVE-E."

Johnny slammed into the refrigerator, knocking off the Spider-Man magnet. "I'm ready, Dad." His heels collapsed the back of his shoes. Johnny wiggled his index finger down and shoehorned his shoe on. Johnny smiled. His two adult front teeth dwarfed his other baby teeth. His freckled face and red hair made him stand out in any group, which he hated, being the smallest boy in his class already.

"It's about damn time," Bill said. Johnny stayed at the far side of the kitchen. Bill had never hit Johnny, but Johnny was taking no chances just the same. "Johnny, eat your bacon and potatoes while I make your lunch."

"I'm not hungry, Dad. Can I just have a banana?"

"No!" Bill said. "Eat what I made you." Bill enjoyed being a dad, but he had never had any boundaries. He tried to be special to Mary and Johnny, but he usually screwed it up. He got out Johnny's Spider-Man lunch box and tossed an apple and juice box into it, made a peanut butter sandwich, and tossed some corn chips into a baggie. An open UPS box was full of Tupperware that Mary had ordered at a party. Bill grabbed a bright red, six-ounce container. When he pushed his thumb against the lid, it didn't move. Both thumbs were indented by the lid before it popped off. Bill looked over to see the back of Johnny's head. He was just staring at his breakfast, making little roads in the hash browns with his fork.

Bill quietly brought the snack container to his bedroom. He took two spring-loaded snakes out of a joke Can-of-Nuts and loaded the snakes into the snack container and pressed on the lid. The lid was clear and did not disguise the snakes. He returned to the kitchen, took a small piece of Saran Wrap and put a teaspoon of applesauce on it. Bill spread the Saran Wrap over the inside of the clear lid with the applesauce showing through the top. Bill again carefully pressed the snakes into the red Tupperware and pressed the lid on. He took a razor blade and trimmed off the exposed Saran Wrap, then held it up to his face, carefully examining it for any flaws. He thought, Johnny will be surprised. It's perfect. "Mary, the kid's ready. Are you gonna get your ass out here and get him to school on time or not?"

She stepped to within inches of Bill, leaned forward with a snarled face, and stuttered, "What... tt... is your problem today?"

Bill stepped back until his back touched the counter top. "Nothing. It's just that I am doing everything."

"Don't give me that shit; you're pissed off about something." Mary paused for five seconds, tapping the brush on the palm of her hand. "How much did you lose?"

"Shit. Mary, don't interrogate me."

"What do you think, that I am an idiot? You didn't say a word to me last night when you got home. You just poured yourself a drink, threw the sports section across the room, and passed out on the couch. I saw this same bullshit for sixteen years from my father. Tell me, how much did you lose?"

"OK, I lost five hundred on a horse. Damn, it's not a big deal." Bill turned his back to Mary and thought, I know she is pissed, but I don't need this pressure now. "I had an inside tip on a horse. She won, too, but was disqualified. It was bullshit."

"Where are we going to get five hundred dollars? PG&E sent us a forty-eight hour notice to pay." Mary turned her back to Bill and took a deep breath. She turned back around and threw her hands into the air. "Hey, you know what? I don't give a shit. Just don't take it out on us." She started to walk back to the bathroom, stopped, and said, "And if you want the car today, drop me off at work. I can't be late again,"

Bill clenched his fist. He wanted to hit something, but turned away. He didn't ever want to be that guy. "Naw, I'm not going anywhere but Kelly's today, but park the car at the far end of the lot. I don't want it to get dinged."

"Well, if that's the case, you can walk Johnny to school. And what time do you get off?"

"Ahhhh, shit! Yeah, OK, at least I'll be able to pick up a decent cup of coffee." Bill emptied his mug into the sink. "It's Monday, so I think Ignacio will close at midnight."

★★★

Bill and Johnny walked down Olive Street under a canopy of magnolia trees that lined both sides of the street, shading them from the sunlight. The tree trunks had outgrown their openings and pushed up the edges of the sidewalk. Johnny dragged his foot to make a trail in the fallen leaves. A block away from the school, Johnny looked around and behind. "Dad, leave me here. I can walk the rest of the way myself."

"Why, do you care what the other kids think?" Bill knew Johnny was picked on and wanted him to stand up for himself. "OK, but I'll walk down the other side of the street."

"Dad, the other kids might see you. Can't you trust me to walk one block to school?"

Bill bent down and put his arms around Johnny, giving him a big squeeze. Johnny squirmed away. Bill said, "All right, you have a choice. I can walk on the other side of the street and hopefully nobody sees me or I can hold your hand all the way to your classroom, and in front of everybody, I will give you a big, wet kiss goodbye."

"Dad, you're so lame."

"I'm not lame," Bill said as he grabbed Johnny by the shoulders.

"Why can't you just be like everyone else's father and let me go by myself?"

"Oh, I guess this means that you want me to walk you to your... ?"

Before Bill had a chance to finish his sentence, Johnny broke in, "All right, you can watch me from across the street."

CHAPTER 4

Bill was desperate about not having the money for Lawrence. It won't do any good not to show up for work, he thought. Ignacio needs me, and Lawrence's boss will be pissed off if he has to come looking for me. He hoped to get lucky. Monday was garbage day on Olive Street, and all the cans were on the curbside. Bill stopped in front of a ranch-style home with a red tiled roof and lifted the lid on the garbage can. Wet coffee grounds sat on top of scraps of food and a black bag. It smelled of curdled milk, so he replaced the lid and moved to the next house. Three doors down was a recycle bin. It had Sunday's paper on top of boxes and more paper. He rummaged through until he found two Nordstrom receipts for cash purchases. One was for two pairs of men's slacks and a man's belt, the second for a cashmere sweater. He smiled and put both receipts in his pocket. Great, he thought, this will take care of Lawrence. Bill continued digging through the can until he found a Nordstrom shopping bag. He neatly folded the bag and put it into his inside pocket, being careful not to crumple it. Next, he walked to Starbucks and ordered a Grande Americano coffee. Back at home, he added Kahlua and brandy. He took the receipts out and sat down at the kitchen table. He got some tissue paper and lightly wadded it up and put it into the Nordstrom bag. The bag now had the appearance of being full. Bill laid down on the couch with the TV remote control; he didn't have to be at work until three.

CHAPTER 5

The stale, sweaty smell in a second-grade classroom is indestructible. It would outlive a thousand power washings, bleaching, and maybe even Lysol. The light noon breeze coming through the open windows only circulated it, combining it with the smell of chalk dust, tempura paints, and fermenting lunches.

Miss Philips stood in front of thirty-two anxious and hungry seven-year-olds. Johnny cleared off his desk and took out his Spider Man lunch box. Mike, sitting behind Johnny, was bored and crumbled a piece of scrap paper into a ball. He popped it into his mouth, chewing it into a drippy wet wad. He waited until Miss Philips wasn't watching and dropped the wad inside Johnny's shirt. When Johnny turned in surprise, Mike pushed the back of the chair, throwing Johnny, the chair, and the lunch box onto the floor. The children around him all laughed just as bell rang. The class was instantly filled with shouting and laughter as the kids rushed to be first out the door to lunch. Johnny sat his desk upright, grabbed his lunch box, and rushed for the door.

Liz Bell pushed Johnny aside so she could catch up with Marsha. Johnny pushed back to hold his ground, as Liz yelled, "Don't touch me. I'll get cooties."

"If I have cooties, I got them from you."

"You're ugly."

"You smell."

"You're stupid."

"You're a dummy," Johnny retorted.

"You're a nincompoop," Liz said.

As Johnny said, "Stupid head," Donnie Callaghan nonchalantly cocked his arm and slugged Johnny on the shoulder to squeeze by him. This pushed Johnny into Liz, and she purposely fell to the floor in very melodramatic fashion, breaking her fall with her extended right arm.

Miss Philips grasped Johnny's arm and scolded Johnny and Liz. "You two stop this right now. Johnny, you tell Liz you're sorry."

Johnny rolled his hazel eyes and whispered, "Sorry."

Miss Philips released her grasp. Liz giggled, looked back at Miss Philips to be sure she wasn't still looking, and stuck her tongue out. They hurried out onto the asphalt schoolyard.

Once outside, the children were the wards of Mrs. Laddy, a long-time parent volunteer who enjoyed being in charge. She was an imposing woman, tall, big boned but not fat, and had her hair pulled back into a tight bun, held together by a pencil. She wore a pleated plaid skirt that neatly hung just below her knees, and a white long-sleeved blouse with a cameo brooch. She could see the battle just inside the door.

Johnny and Liz were still pushing each other as they filed out the door. Mrs. Laddy grabbed Johnny by the back of his shirt and led him to the end of the bench right by the classroom door, and said, "Hey, young man, you quit that right now. I want you to sit on the bench here where I can keep an eye on you."

Johnny sat down on the bench without a word and scooted over next to his best friend Jason. He waited until Mrs. Laddy was out of earshot, then turned to Jason and said, "Liz is a butthead. She tried to get me in trouble. I'm gonna get her."

"Yeah, she's stupid. I hate her too," Jason replied.

"Donnie slugged me in the arm, that jerk," Johnny said as he rubbed his shoulder.

"This morning, Mike put me in a head lock and gave me a noogie until I gave him my Snickers," Jason said. Johnny and Jason hated that they had to endure punishment from the class bullies Mike and Donnie.

Johnny turned his Spider Man lunch box upside down to inspect the bottom and thought, You can never be too careful. Dad could have put something on it.

Johnny never knew what he might find in his lunch box. His father enjoyed surprising him whenever he could. Bill had previously put a can of dog food, a baby bottle, and nutty embarrassing notes taped to the bottom of his lunch box that Johnny wouldn't see but that those seated across from him would. Last week, Bill saw a basket of mushrooms in the refrigerator and put them into his lunch, still with the plastic wrap rubber banded over the top. Mrs. Laddy saw the mushrooms and made Johnny eat every one of them.

She wouldn't believe that it had been just a joke, telling him, "If your father put this into your lunch, then he wants you to eat it."

Johnny pleaded with Mrs. Laddy that they were making him sick, but Mrs. Laddy was relentless and responded, "Nobody leaves the bench until they've eaten all their lunch!"

Johnny was very upset, but Bill brushed off the incident. "Mrs. Laddy is an idiot!" was Bill's only comment.

When he opened the pail, the Thermos had squashed the peanut butter sandwich. Johnny carefully peeled back the top slice of squished bread and created a brick pathway of Frito's corn chips. Julia Child would marvel at this creation. While his mouth was still full of the sticky peanut butter, he pulled the straw off the side of his juice box, punched it into the top, and sucked the juice almost dry in one continuous gulp.

Johnny stuffed the second half of the sandwich into his mouth in one piece, pushing his cheeks out like a squirrel. He now looked into the lunch box, picked up the apple, took a close look at it, and handed it to Jason. Johnny then grabbed the bright red Tupperware with both hands and pushed his thumbs under the edge of the cover. The hard new plastic was stiff and would not yield. Johnny inspected the top to see the applesauce that awaited him inside. He pried as hard as he could, but it only stabbed into his fingers, leaving deep imprints into his thumbs. Mrs. Laddy was keeping close watch on Johnny and could see the strain in his face as he struggled with the top.

"Would you like me to open it for you?" Mrs. Laddy asked.

Johnny couldn't talk. He still had a mouth full of bread and peanut butter.

"Don't you know that it's rude not to answer when I ask you a question?"

Johnny still couldn't swallow the sandwich, but instead reached his hand out with the container. Mrs. Laddy took the Tupperware with her right hand while holding her can of Coke in her left. She pushed her thumb against the lid, but it didn't budge. As she pushed harder, she only made her finger hurt. Mrs. Laddy put her soda under her left armpit to free both hands. The lid popped away and applesauce and plastic snakes rocketed out. Mrs. Laddy jumped back screaming as she threw the Tupperware. The Coke dropped to the asphalt, exploding on Mrs. Laddy, Johnny, and Jason. The peanut butter, bread, and chips projected from Johnny's mouth onto Mrs. Laddy's legs. Fifteen children all screamed at the same time. Lunch boxes, sandwiches, and drinks all went flying. Mrs. Laddy had Johnny's sandwich on her legs, soda on her face and hair, and Marsha's milk on her skirt. Quickly, the screaming turned to laughter from all the boys and girls.

"This is not funny!" Mrs. Laddy screamed. "Johnny Giovanni, look at this mess! You are a horrible little brat.

You clean up this *damn* mess now! Then I am taking you to the principal's office."

A deafening silence ended the commotion. Mrs. Laddy was panting, her face red, trying to catch her breath. Nobody had ever heard her swear before.

CHAPTER 6

At one in the afternoon, Bill got off the couch, took a shower, shaved, grabbed the Nordstrom bag, and left. At Nordstrom, he went straight to the men's department. The store was almost empty of customers. At the slack display, he discreetly examined each sales tag. He quickly found the first pair of slacks that matched his receipt and put them into the bag. The second pair of slacks wasn't there.

A salesman approached, and Bill felt his heart pound. "Hello, sir, is there anything I can help you with?" the man asked.

Bill pulled the bag close to him, "Oh no, I'm just browsing. Are these all the slacks you have?"

"You might want to check the ones we have on clearance. They're in the center aisle."

"Thank you, I'll check them out." Bill circled the clearance display.

A sales girl came up and asked, "Can I help you, sir?"

"Just looking, thank you."

Bill found the second pair of slacks. The clearance table had wool sweaters, where he found the blue cashmere V-neck sweater listed on the receipt. At the accessories department, he found what he was looking for. He put the belt into the bag and headed for the escalator before another salesman was able to assist him.

The sound of "As Time Goes By" flowed from atop the escalator. Julie, a young woman in her mid-twenties, was playing a Yamaha piano. Her long, blond hair hung down her back. Bill stared at a rose tattoo as it moved with her breast, veiled by a white lace top that hung from her shoulders by two delicate ribbons. Her long fingers danced effortlessly across the keyboard.

"Oh, wow, I've always wanted a piano but I've never had the room till now," Bill said, as the last notes of the song trailed off.

Julie's looked up to see him staring at her. She pulled her blouse and fastened the top button.

Bill continued: "I just made an offer on a fourteen-room Victorian that I want to fix up. This piano would be great in the parlor under the stained glass dome."

"Your family must really like the house," Julie said.

"Oh no, I'm not married. I just love old houses, and this house is in foreclosure, so I am getting a great deal."

Julie responded, "What do you do for a living?"

"I work for a Wall Street venture capital firm." Bill ran his hand through his hair. "I'm the one who funded My Spot Dot Com. Now they want me out here in Silicon Valley. They are trying to compete with the Sand Hill Road VCs and that is why they sent me here. I love the weather."

"Oh, that's exciting. Do you know that this is also a player piano?"

Bill sat on the edge of the piano's bench. "No, I didn't even know that they still made players anymore. This is so cool. Show me how it works."

Julie, feeling crowded by Bill, moved away to the opposite edge of the bench. "I'm not keeping you from anything?"

"Oh no," Bill said, "I have an appointment with my Realtor in an hour. The house is in the center of the downtown district on McKinley Street, and I'm going to love living so close to where all the night life is."

"I hope you enjoy your house."

"I will, but tell me more about this player. Is there much music available for it?"

"Oh, we have hundreds of discs for it. And what's really cool is you can make your own disc. Like, if you have a friend who likes to jam, you can record whatever he plays on a disc."

"Do you enjoy jam sessions yourself?" Bill asked.

Julie looked around and said, "I do sometimes, but I hardly ever have time anymore."

Bill looked around, and not seeing anyone, said, "Am I keeping you too long?"

"Oh, that's OK. I was just checking," Julie replied. "I can't afford to lose this job."

Bill, with a big smile on his face, asked, "Do you ever have time to just go out for drink? I don't work this Thursday if you want to meet?"

Julie looked directly into Bills eyes and said, "That sounds like fun, but like I said, I don't have any free time."

"Can I call you?"

Julie paused, then said, "I don't give my number out to strangers, but maybe I will run into you again."

"That's OK." Bill looked at his watch. "I have to go see my Realtor."

Julie noticed the worn finish of the fake Rolex.

Bill walked despondently toward the escalator, looked back at Julie, and said, "I'll stop by again."

Julie rolled her eyes.

He returned to the men's accessory counter and presented his bag of returns to the sales clerk. "My wife bought these for my birthday and I don't really like them. I have the receipts and would like my money back." Bill placed both receipts on the counter and the two pairs of pants, the sweater, and the belt.

The salesman cheerfully responded, "Oh that will be fine. It'll only take a few minutes." He scanned each item into the register, "The total comes to $565.62, sir. Would you like store credit or a cash refund?"

"I would like the cash, please," Bill said.

As the clerk counted out the cash to Bill, he said, "Is there anything else I can help you with?"

"Thank you but not today," Bill said, as he walked away.

The salesman called to Bill, "Thank you for shopping at Nordstrom, please come again."

★★★

At Kelly's Bar, Ignacio stood on a stool with a feather duster, carefully circling each bottle and piece of memorabilia. He wore a blue apron protecting his new dress shirt. Charlie was sitting at the bar, sipping chardonnay. "Make sure you don't get any of that dust into my wine."

"Very funny," Ignacio said as he dusted two framed newspapers with the headlines:

Rookie Kelly KO's Rocco in 12th
Kidnappers Lynched

"That's the hundredth time you told me that."

As Bill walked into the bar, he said to Ignacio, "I got here a little early if you're ready to go home."

"That would be nice, Bill; I am a little worn out from cleaning." Ignacio stepped off the stool and untied his apron. "You and Charlie were pretty unlucky last night."

"We got screwed by the officials," Bill replied. "Shady Sis won that race."

Charlie sipped his wine. "You were right about Shady Sis; she won the race by a mile."

Bill stood behind the counter and said to Ignacio, "You're getting too old for this. Retire already."

Ignacio walked toward the door. "Who would keep you out of trouble if I wasn't here? You haven't changed in twenty years."

"Ha, ha. It's me who needs to watch out for you!" Bill picked up the empty wine glass. "Charlie, are you ready for another?"

"Not wine, though; make it an Old Fashioned and put some booze in it this time, will ya?"

Bill smiled. "Shit, Charlie, I make them so strong now that your piss will be at least a hundred proof."

"Like hell you do," Charlie said. "I make my granddaughter's Shirley Temples stronger than this."

"Is that why she is so easy?" Bill said.

"You asshole," Charlie barked.

"Do you want a double?"

"Yeah, sure."

The door opened and Charlie and Bill turned to watch Florence sashay her seductive six-foot body up to a bar stool. Her low-cut white blouse showed off her cleavage. Bill set an Old Fashioned on the bar. Charlie quickly removed the cherry and flipped it into the ashtray and said, "You're the only FUCKIN' ASSHOLE in this town who still knows how to make an Old Fashioned."

Bill didn't answer but instead turned to Florence and said, "You're so damn sexy I'll buy *you* a drink. What do you want?"

Florence replied in a slow, Southern drawl, "Now that's the best offer I've had all day. How about a martini?"

"How about me with your martini? You'll never want anyone else," Bill said, as he took a martini glass from the freezer. The glass was coated on the inside with crushed ice. When Bill poured the gin from the shaker, the ice became translucent and sparkled like diamonds.

Florence replied, "You keep trying, I'll give you that, but the man I want has to have a brain."

Bill said, "A big dick is more fun."

Charlie laughed. "You've been trying to impress women with that act since you started bartending." He set his glass down. "Has it ever worked?"

"All the time," Bill said, as he put Florence's martini on the counter.

Hippie Paul, a sixty-year-old man with worn, patched blue jeans and a red plaid flannel shirt walked in. He had been coming regularly for two years. Nobody knew him well, but he always ordered a pitcher of Anchor Steam beer and took it to a back booth to drink while he typed on his Apple laptop. An hour later, he would order a second pitcher and type for two more hours. He never left a tip. If it wasn't for the computer, Bill would've thought he was a bum. His hair was shoulder length, tangled and oily. His beard always had a couple of days' growth.

"A pitcher of Anchor, please."

"How's it going?" Bill asked.

"OK," he responded without making eye contact. "Thank you."

Bill handed him the pitcher of beer and carried the glass and a basket of peanuts to the empty booth in the back. The customer slid in and poured himself a full glass, drank half of it, cracked and ate four peanuts, and began to type. For two years this routine had always been the same. By the time Bill returned to behind the bar, everyone was quietly sipping their drinks. He knew how to get Charlie riled up.

"Hey, Charlie, did you vote in the primary today?"

"Who the fuck do you mistake me for, a pansy ass sucker who believes that we actually have a say in our government? They're all a bunch of sexual perverts who have their mitts in our pocket." Charlie pounded his clenched fist on the bar.

Bill said, "And do you let him play with your balls when he puts his hand in your pockets?"

"You asshole! Give me some more peanuts."

★★★

The dim bar lit up when the door opened, allowing the bright Santa Clara Valley sunlight to flood in. Bill and Charlie turned to see Lawrence in the doorway. "Hey, you look like you're having a great time. What's the big occasion?" Lawrence, a tall black man, wore bright blue jogging sweats, a heavy braided gold chain around his neck, and an Oakland Raiders ball cap. "Did someone win the lottery?" He walked up to the bar and high-fived Bill and Charlie.

"What's up, Lawrence?" Bill asked.

"You white boy's will never get it right," Lawrence said, laughing. "Shady Sis gave you guys a good tease, but in the end she let you down."

"We were screwed," Bill said. "She won the race. DAMN!"

"Come on bro, what are you complaining about? You only lost five Franklins. Charlie here lost twenty. You don't see him crying in his drink."

Bill poured an Anchor Steam beer from the tap and placed it on the bar. "I know; it's not the five hundred that I'm pissed off about. It's what I should have won. Fifteen grand!"

"OK," Lawrence said, as he picked up the mug and drank it half down. "You should have never turned me on to Anchor. It's the best damn beer I've ever had. Now I'm spoiled, but it's too expensive for a poor man like me."

"Poor boy, shit!" Bill said. "You're walking out of here with twenty-five hundred dollars. Did you forget that?"

"You need to chill. I'm just a little guy, the messenger." Lawrence put his thumb and index finger a quarter inch apart. "I only get a teeny little split. You're the one who gets big fat tips all day from drunks. You interested in another pony today?"

Bill looked at Charlie. "I've been burned by the horses already. How about the Giants' game tonight, Charlie? Are you interested? Woody is pitching tonight, against Perez at Pac Bell."

Charlie looked up at Lawrence and asked, "What are the odds?"

Lawrence pulled out a three-by-four-inch spiral notebook, studied it, and said, "Dodgers, by one run."

Bill said, "Woody is the money man, are you in?"

"Yah," Charlie answered. "Put me down for a Franklin. How about you, Bill?"

"OK, baseball I understand. I'll go for a Franklin, too," Bill said, as he reached into his pocket and pulled out the money he got from Nordstrom. Charlie placed twenty hundred dollar bills on the bar, which Lawrence picked up.

Lawrence finished his beer. "Thanks for the brew and good luck on them Giants tonight."

In the back booth, the hippy tossed a peanut into his mouth, cracked it between his teeth, and spit the shell on the floor. He typed and grabbed for the mug but missed the handle, splashing some beer on his laptop. In his effort to quickly upright the mug, he inhaled the peanut still in his mouth. As he gasped for air, he knew he was in trouble. He felt the peanut deep in his throat. His heart was pounding as he tried to stand up, but the table blocked him. He didn't have the strength to slide from the inside of the booth. His face turned a deep purple. He raised his hand but the wall of the booth shielded him from everyone's sight. He struggled as he slowly slid back down into the leather seat.

As afternoon became evening, the booze kept flowing, and the arguments grew louder. Bill walked to the back to see why the hippy hadn't gotten his second pitcher. Hippie Paul's white, stiff body was draped down the booth, his eyes open and staring into Bill's face. Bill felt dizzy as vomit erupted up the back of his throat. He held his stomach and swallowed the burning vomit. Bill touched him to confirm that he was dead.

He immediately pulled his hand back when he felt the cold cheek. Bill picked up his laptop computer, closed it, and discreetly put it under the bar before he called 911.

CHAPTER 7

November 24, 1933

The new Dreamland Auditorium was packed. The majestic building was host to balls, ice shows, conventions, and, tonight, boxing. Temporary seating had been added on the floor surrounding the twenty-foot square ring. John Kelly sat on a three-legged stool, drenched in sweat and blood. His construction-strong arms glistened. Exhausted from eleven rounds, he couldn't speak as Pete wiped his blond hair and barreled chest with a wet towel.

"You are the best sparring partner I have ever had at the gym. This might be your first fight, but you got Rocco where you want him. He's running on fumes; he's never gone this far. Just wait and you will find your spot."

John thought about how he boxed with his brother, Michael, in his pop's basement. Pop had given them gloves to make sure they could take care of themselves, and John could easily beat his older brother by the time he was twelve.

The bell rang and the wood bleachers shook and rattled. The Friday night crowd screamed as their favorite, Rocco Cancio, stood up. The North Beach Italians were here to see their native son qualify for a possible title fight. Rocco seemed unbeatable; he had won all ten previous fights by knockouts, all within six rounds. John attacked forward, but the taller Rocco landed another blow to John's face.

John kept his arms up, though his eyebrow was split open and his body was badly bruised. Warm blood blurred his vision and dripped onto his bright green boxing trunks. He attacked again and Rocco landed two more punches into his face, but he wasn't thrown backwards this time. John moved inside and delivered three hard body blows. He fended off Rocco's jabs using the ropes to leverage his weight and keep balance. John's blood and sweat sprayed onto the spectators behind him after Rocco landed another punch.

John was determined. He had been knocked down in the second and ninth rounds and was far behind in the scoring. Damned if I'm going let a wop beat me. I can do this; I am much stronger. John had his future riding on this fight. The winning purse was five hundred dollars, but John had also bet his entire savings of seven hundred dollars at three-to-one odds on himself winning.

John threw three left jabs that Rocco blocked with his gloves, but he didn't move his feet. Pete's plan was working. He felt a rush; his arms felt light and his feet danced. Rocco threw a combination of punches that John fended off. John could feel Rocco's frustration. This was supposed to be just a tune-up fight for him before a possible title match. John kept his wide shoulders pinned against the ropes, giving him balance as Rocco threw a wild right punch. John moved his head to the left as the punch harmlessly brushed by his right ear. Rocco's momentum threw him sideways into John just as John threw a powerful right blow to Rocco's midsection. Rocco stumbled backwards. John sprang forward off the ropes, hitting Rocco with four quick jabs. Rocco covered up with his arms in front of his face. John slammed another right blow into Rocco's stomach, completely knocking the wind out of him. Over the roar of the crowd, John heard a rib crack. Rocco collapsed to the mat with a deafening thud. The referee slowly counted one... two... three... as the crowd screamed, "Get UP Rocco, get up!"

The referee held John's arm up, declaring him the winner by knockout. John left the ring, the booing echoing as Pete escorted him up the auditorium aisle. John's head was thrown back as an apple exploded on his cheek. He tried to jog up the aisle, but his legs ached. Blood, sweat, beer, and crushed apple covered him by the time he found relief in the dressing room.

The next morning, a cool, fog-wet wind swept across the ship repair docks. A fishing boat edged close to the docks to avoid the strong flood tide. Its bow wave rocked the sailboats in the slips. The forty-foot fishing boat was no match for San Francisco's strong tide. It barely inched forward in a quest to get out of the narrow Golden Gate Strait.

Daniel Kelly carried a long, wooden toolbox packed with chisels, saws, hammers, and large block planes. He wore heavy wool pants and a carpenter's work jacket with a watch pocket, pencil slot, and large buttoned pockets for holding small hand tools. His son John wore a cypress green and brown tweed coat with a red polka-dotted kerchief accenting the breast pocket. His tie material matched the kerchief. The freshly stitched cut on John's eyebrow was red and still oozing. Both eyes were black, and his face was swollen. There were ten other passengers at the Southern Pacific Train Station on Townsend Street waiting to get on the 8:45 to San Jose. One little blond-haired boy stared at John while he clung to his mother's leg.

The train bellowed black coal smoke and steam as it pulled out of the station. Daniel and John were on their way to Sunnyvale. To the left, the fog horn echoed. Within minutes, the industrial buildings of the city disappeared. The fog lingered, hiding all but one row of the headstones in Colma's cemeteries. The sun finally broke out over the emerald rolling hills of Mill's dairy in Millbrae. As the train traveled south, the weather warmed a little and the sky cleared. Endless orchards of vibrant fruit-bearing trees surrounded occasional hamlets of homes and shops.

Jerome, Harold, and Lou, Sunnyvale locals, passed around a hand-rolled cigarette while standing on the corner of Murphy Street and Evelyn Avenue outside Wilson's Feed and Supply. The window displayed shovels, smudge pots, horse shoes, blankets, brushes, and a milking machine. Harold tucked his thumb under a thick, braided tan and gray hemp rope coiled over his left shoulder. He had lost his farm to the bank a year ago. His younger brother, Jerome, dressed in slacks, a wool sport jacket, and a tan driving cap, had recently quit college to find work. Lou took the cigarette with both hands to steady his shaking as he inhaled. He was a machinist at the Hendy Iron Works until it stopped production three months ago. Yesterday, they were able to only able to work loading and tying down bales of hay for two dollars per truckload.

Steam from the approaching San Francisco train rose into the sky. Just across the gravel railway, the Del Monte, Libby's, and Shultz canneries were closed until summer. This clear, chilly November morning, there were only a few souls walking on the sidewalk. A stout young man, eyes half hidden by his fedora's bent brim, approached the three and said, "Hey, Lou, are they OK?"

Lou responded, "Yeah, they're OK, but not today."

The man tipped his hat and continued up the street.

"Who was that?" Harold asked.

"He's just a bootlegger, but that's the last bottle of gin I will buy from him. It made me sick all night."

"That's a good one," Jerome said. "Blame it on the gin. I'll have to remember that line for the next time I tie one on and puke my guts out." Jerome and Harold both pushed at Lou's shoulder and laughed.

John and Daniel had arrived in the Valley for a grand weekend. John had purchased tickets for the big game between Cal and Stanford that afternoon. Sunday would be the christening of Colleen, the baby of John's sister Patricia, at St. Joseph's in San Jose. John was to be the godfather. But first, they had business to attend to; John hoped to get his father's blessing.

Sunnyvale Train Station about 1933
Courtesy of Sunnyvale Historical Collection

"We need to hurry, Pop, the special Game Train leaves in two hours."

Daniel combed his thick, white hair straight back. A master carpenter, he came to San Francisco immediately after the Great San Francisco Earthquake of 1906. An accomplished woodcarver by the age of fifteen, he'd chiseled ornate statues for English churches. He learned his trade as an indentured servant for an English carpenter in Ireland.

They walked two blocks up Murphy Avenue and nodded to the three men standing in front of the hardware store. They stopped in the middle of the street to examine a boarded-up building. The paint was peeling off the cracked, weathered siding. Painted in faded red letters on the dusty window was *Brigitte's Grocery & Supply.* At the bottom of the window it read, *Fresh Meats - Groceries - Block Ice.* The door had an official notice of a sale date taped to it. They looked in to see that all the shelves were bare.

John held his arms up with a big smile on his battered face. "Pop, I told you this is a great spot for a bar... it even has a walk-in ice-box! The entire downtown is just up the street, and in a couple of weeks all these men who work here will be wanting a place to wet their whistle. We will have just have less than two weeks to get it opened. Do you think we can do it?"

"'Twas a fine building once, laddie. It could be fixed into a fine bar, but what good 'tis if you can't get a license?" Daniel crossed his arms. "You should think about this awhile. You are doing pretty good working for me, so why take the risk?"

"Because, Pop, I'm not a craftsman like you. I hate living in the city waiting for a summer that never comes." John placed his hands on top of his head, turned a full circle, and looked into the sky for half a minute, trying to calm his frustration. "I fought a fight to do this. Besides, Patrick moved Patricia down here to keep her away from us. I don't trust him."

Daniel placed his arm around John. "You're a good brother to Patricia. I'll feel better knowing you're here to protect her, laddie." He looked behind to see that no one could hear him and said, "You're not doing this just to get away from that Jezebel, are ya?"

"No, Pop, we should have never gotten married… I just couldn't make her happy." John turned and looked at the store. "I just need to do this."

"I just want you to give me grandchildren someday, John."

"Well, Pop, I don't think that will ever happen but Michael and Patricia have given you four already." He quickly changed the subject. "The foreclosure sale is Monday morning. I just hope there aren't any other bidders."

"Oh, Johnny, haven't I ever told ya that if ya buy what you don't need, ya may have to sell what ya do?"

"Pop, you've been telling me that my whole life. I already applied for a liquor license. Prohibition ends in two weeks and I want to be open and throw a party. This will be the first bar in Sunnyvale."

The three men heard John's last statement. They introduced themselves with robust handshaking. Jerome lifted his driving cap and said, "My hat's off to any man who wants to open a bar in Sunnyvale. Don't worry about business; my friends and I will keep you plenty busy."

Harold added, "My friend Lou here has a particular hankering for bootleg gin; don't ya, Lou?"

Lou turned his shaking head down. "I won't ever drink gin again, but I guess you have some fine Irish whiskey."

John said, "I could use some now; my entire body hurts."

A shadow moved slowly down the street until the entire block was in the dark. Lou felt chilled and looked up, expecting to see a cloud. "Holy cow, look at the size of that sucker!" The five of them looked up in the chilled air to see the long-awaited arrival of the dirigible *USS Macon*. The *USS Macon* was built to defend the West Coast from any surprise attack from the expanding Japanese empire. It was a flying aircraft carrier with five Sparrow hawk fighter biplanes inside. It silently glided fifty feet over the rooftops toward the bay. The internal aluminum frame protruded like ribs into the dope-coated fabric skin. It extended the length of seven storefronts and was as tall as the two-story Grizzo Market.

"How can something that big stay up in the sky? It's bigger than a football field," John said. "It's against the law of gravity."

Lou said, "I heard it has seventy-five men aboard."

Sunday evening, John and Daniel splurged at the Hotel De Anza in downtown San Jose. Daniel had built the curved, walnut handrails for the lobby staircase a few years ago, but he had never been in the hotel to see them installed. Saint James Square sat between the beautiful Art Deco hotel and the courthouse where the foreclosure sale would be held. There were six properties to be sold on the courthouse steps at nine o'clock on Monday morning.

USS Macon By USN—US NAVAL HISTORICAL CENTER Photo #: 80-G-462246

Nine-thirty Sunday evening, John and Daniel raised their glasses of whiskey. "To Colleen, my god-daughter and your granddaughter," John said.

"Tis a beautiful lassie, she is," Daniel added. "She has flaming red hair like her mother."

They continued toasting Colleen with two more shots of whiskey. When the bartender opened a new bottle, they decided to toast the Stanford Indians, who had defeated the Cal Bears seven to three the day before. The speakeasy was in a basement below Woolworth's Five and Dime. The top twelve inches of wall on the street side had wired frosted windows that opened onto the outside sidewalk. Hanging on the wall behind the bar was a ceiling-high oil painting of a naked Eve reaching for the apple on the forbidden tree. A damp, musty smell hung in the room that never saw sunlight. A circular chandelier illuminated the bar; its crystal droplet beads broke the light into miniature rainbows.

A tense mood hung in the room, as an unexploded bomb was ticking just outside. Prohibition and the Great Depression was a time of lawlessness. San Jose was a small city, the agriculture center of about fifty thousand. Alex Hart owned Hart's Department Store, the largest retailer in the county. He was active in the community and known for his generosity. His son, Brock, a popular sports star at the University of Santa Clara, had recently graduated and was to assume the responsibility of taking over the business. He was good looking with wavy, blond hair, and everyone noticed when he drove by in his new, light green Studebaker Roadster convertible. Two weeks earlier, Brock had been kidnapped and killed; the town was enraged. It made headlines every day throughout the state. Governor Rolph encouraged retribution by sternly stating publicly, "I will pardon anyone involved in their lynching."

The men at the bar carried on a loud discussion about the jailed murderers of Brock Hart. One boasted, "They oughta slowly burn them."

Another smashed his fist into his open hand. "That's too good for them! Let me at 'em; I'll make them wish they were just hung."

Two couples sat at a small table listening to the radio. The sultry voice of Ethel Waters was singing "Stormy

Weather." "She is down because she lost her man" could be heard during lulls in the shouting.

"Fifteen-two, Fifteen-four and a pair is eight," John said to his father as he moved a peg forward on the cribbage board.

Two classmates of Brock, Sam Hawkins and former child actor Jackie Coogan, burst through the door, allowing the roar from the growing mob to be heard. Jackie headed quickly to the radio, yelling, "We're going to lynch them tonight."

He changed the station to KQW and turned the volume up. Radio host Sam Hayes broadcasted, "Come on down to see a lynching; these cowards are going to be hung tonight. Hurry down to Saint James Square in San Jose. They are moving them to San Francisco tonight and we deserve revenge."

John stood up but could only see the flashes of headlights through the ceiling windows. Lou and Harold ran into the bar, spreading the word. Harold still had his rope over his shoulder. Lou spotted John and said, "Hey John, did you hear what's happening in the park?"

"Hi, Lou; what's going on?"

Lou pointed his hand toward the square. "They're in the jail right over there! It's happening tonight."

Daniel stood up and put his hand on John's back. "'Tis an ugly brood out there. 'Tis not our place to meddle in this."

"Thanks, Pop, but I need to see what's going to happen." John hurriedly followed Lou and Harold out the door into the square.

The kidnappers, Harold Thurmond and Jack Holmes, were in the small city jail just on the other side of Saint James Square. A growing crowd had been keeping vigil since Brock's body was found in the marshes of the bay's shore on Friday, shot multiple times. The crowd had quickly grown into a mob; car headlights lit up the square. There were thousands filling the square and all of the connecting streets. A half-dozen men ran through the crowd, yelling, "Lynch them, lynch them!" They surrounded the jailhouse on the edge of the square. The police locked themselves in the jailhouse as men carried bricks from a nearby construction site and threw them through every window.

John turned to Lou and said, "I can't believe they really might do this... it's murder! Why don't the paddies break it up?"

"There aren't enough of them," Lou held his rope in his hand. "They deserve it!"

Someone in the crowd yelled, "The San Francisco police are on their way to move them to the city. We have to do it now."

John looked at Lou in disbelief. As he backed away, he was knocked to the grass by twenty men running, carrying a steel I-beam under their arms. John stayed on the lawn as his head was still spinning from the pounding it took on Friday. He was trapped in the mob and could hear the deep crash every time the I-beam was rammed into the steel jailhouse door. It took great effort to continue pushing the heavy I-beam up the steep stairs to ram the door. The crowd encouraged the men, "Again, again, again." They coordinated each chant every thirty seconds as the I-beam's impact echoed through the square.

John worked his way to the knoll under an elm tree where he could see. Why aren't the San Francisco police here yet? he thought.

After about ten minutes, the door gave way and the mob rushed into the jail. Harold Thurmond and John Holms were dragged down the concrete stairs by their feet, screaming for their lives. "Please don't kill me; don't string me up; don't string me up!" Harold Thurmond screamed, as two farm boys kicked him and six more men joined in tearing his clothes off.

Men and women burned his body with cigars, matches, and cigarettes. One young woman in a red full-length coat poured the contents of her drink glass on Thurmond's pubic hair and lit it on fire. The frenzied crowd cheered, "Torture them, torture them!" Both men were dragged by their feet toward John.

John watched as two ropes were thrown over branches of elm trees. Thurmond appeared unconscious. The woman in the red coat squeezed in between the men, yelling, "We need to wake him up." She poured more liquid on his face until he appeared awake. "I'm not going to let you sleep through this; I want you to suffer."

The noose was put over Thurmond's head and he was pulled up until his naked and burned body was twenty feet overhead. Thurmond hung motionless as if he were a cow's carcass in a slaughterhouse.

Naked, Holmes was being held upright by three men, forced to watch his friend die. He still had fight in him and struggled. They pulled so hard on his hair that some ripped off his scalp. He was punched repeatedly as they forced him under the elm tree. He futilely tossed his head, trying to avoid the noose. He grabbed the noose just as they started pulling the rope. The limb was thick. A dozen men in unison heaved one pull at a time until he was near the top.

Holmes resisted. He reached the rope above his head and pulled himself up. Just as he tried to grab onto the branch, the men below released the rope. Holmes crashed to the ground. Harold grabbed his arm and pulled it behind his back, a loud snap echoing as Holmes screamed.

John Kelly could see the tan and gray hemp rope being pulled up again until Holmes was swinging twenty feet above the ground; this time he just hung motionless.

John walked back to the hotel, where he found Daniel. "Let's go back to our room. I can't stay here; I'm going to be sick," he declared.

Daniel said, "Those bastards' souls are burnin' in hell now. They were never even given a chance to confess their sins."

Postcard of 1933 lynching of Thurmond and Holmes

The next morning, the courthouse square was covered in broken glass and bricks. Newspaper reporters took pictures and interviewed police officers and spectators alike. The morning *Mercury News* headlined Governor Rolph saying, "The best lesson ever given to the county! I would like to release all kidnappers in San Quentin to the fine, patriotic citizens of San Jose." Not a single person was even questioned by the police.

That morning, the auction started an hour late. Only five bidders showed up, but there were two spectators at the bottom of the steps: an older woman trying to keep warm in a brown wool coat and a very young dark-skinned man. John noticed his intense, deep-set eyes and sensed the concern behind them.

California is a deed of trust state, a law left over from when it was part of Spain. The creditor can only set the auction price at what is owed to him. Any amounts above that went to either junior lien holders or the property owner being foreclosed on.

The auctioneer called, "all bidders come forward," and they stepped up one at a time to show the auctioneer the funds for their bid. John Kelly, with Daniel by his side, counted out twenty hundred dollar bills carefully so as not to let anyone other than the auctioneer see the cash. The auctioneer wrote the name of each bidder and the amount of cash they brought in a pocket notebook. After the other four bidders were done, he announced, "I will start the bidding for each property with the minimum bid given to me by the creditor. You may bid on any property up to the amount of funds you brought with you."

The first property auctioned was a three-bedroom house in San Jose. The auctioneer opened the bidding at five hundred and twelve dollars.

"Five hundred thirteen dollars," the gentleman in a gray suit said.

"Five hundred fifty dollars," a farmer in coveralls shouted.

The bidding continued between the two until the man in the gray suit said, "Six hundred fifty dollars."

The auctioneer asked, "Any other bids?" There was silence as the two bidders looked at each other. "Going once, going twice, sold to Mr. Pierce for six hundred fifty dollars."

The farmer shook his head as he walked away.

The second property was a thirty-acre fruit ranch in Gilroy. The opening bid was one thousand five hundred dollars. There was bidding between three men until the property was sold for two thousand three hundred dollars.

John was becoming nervous. He put his hand in his pocket to feel the money he had with him for the bidding. Sweat covered his bruised face and he looked to his pop, who looked back to say, "Laddie, have faith in God. If 'tis meant to be, it will be."

The diner was the third property auctioned. The auctioneer opened the bid at one thousand two hundred ninety-seven dollars. John looked around with clenched fists, examining the other bidders. "I will open the bidding."

The auctioneer called, "Are there any other bids?"

Mr. Pierce and two other men stood on either side of John and Daniel. Mr. Pierce was a local banker who filed the default sales on both the house and the grocery store. He was a regular at foreclosure sales, taking advantage of his customers' hard times. He raised his hand and bid, "One thousand four hundred dollars."

John squeezed the two thousand dollars he had brought. "One thousand four hundred fifty dollars."

Mr. Pierce immediately rose his hand while saying, "One thousand six hundred dollars."

John regretted his pop's advice to not bring all his funds. *"Laddie, you will need some money to fix the place up and to stock it."* John stuck his hand up. "One thousand seven hundred dollars."

John was afraid to look into the eyes of the remaining bidders. The auctioneer asked, "Are there any other bids?" To John, the silence lasted for an eternity. "Going once, twice, sold to Mr. Kelly for one thousand seven hundred dollars."

John turned and hugged his father at the top of the courthouse steps and shouted, "We got it!" At the bottom, he could see the young man with deep eyes he had noticed earlier, with his arm around the woman as they walked away.

CHAPTER 8

December 3, 1933

They had spent the past two weeks tearing out the store's shelving and counters and building a new, grand carved bar. John had been collecting materials to build his dream bar for three years. Labor was cheap but materials were invaluable in remote San Francisco. Laborers straightened used nails and saved every piece of scrap wood left on a job site. John and his pop had worked long days and nights; they wanted this bar to last a lifetime. The wall cabinet behind the bar he built from black walnut with glass shelves. He crowned the top with an ornate hand-carved relief of cherubs, leprechauns, and satyrs surrounding a reclining nude nymph. Daniel trimmed the top edge with copper then said to John, "We need to patina the copper to make it a beautiful Irish green."

"How are you going to do that, Pop?"

"I'm not, you are going to do it."

"I don't know how, Pop."

"It's easy, son; you just need to coat it with your piss."

"What!"

"That's how they did it on the ancient castles. The poor would sell their piss to do it unless they were too poor to have a pot to piss in."

John pissed into a can and brushed it onto the copper. In a few minutes it started turning green. "Pop, I never thought it would work."

"OK, stopped admiring your piss work and let's get back to making the bar." Daniel laughed as he drank some tea.

The countertop had to withstand spilled beer, pounding, fights, drunkard's puke, and cigarette burns. Teak is used on ship decks because it withstands the extreme elements of the sea and the punishment of cargo being dropped and dragged on it. The second day of sanding the hard teak planks, John stopped to re-sharpen the blade of the block plane. The file slipped, cutting deep into the flesh of his calloused palm. "Damn!" The blood poured onto the bar top while he grabbed a rag and wrapped it around the cut. He secured the bandage with masking tape.

Daniel wiped up the mess. "You are only missing the tears to have built your bar with blood, sweat, and tears. You're not looking to go home, are ya?"

"The blood is staining the bar, Pop."

Daniel shook his head. "It is just a speck of color in the wood." He grabbed a steel wool pad soaked with tung oil and polished the bar top. The wood came to life with a beautiful golden grain worthy to be in the finest of establishments.

The bar was taking shape, but John worried about stocking the bar by Monday. Prohibition outlawed the sale of liquor, and most manufactures were out of business. A few distributors survived producing other products. The Anchor Brewery in San Francisco, closed for ten years, had restarted production of Steam Beer last April. John was only able to stock the bar with whisky, gin, and beer in time for the opening. "I don't know what to do, Pop. We open tomorrow night."

"Laddie, be content with what you have. 'Tis a fool who worries 'bout the things he can't change." Daniel put his arm over John's back and said, "I've made a pretty good living makin' quality woodwork. I've sampled your stock plenty. That Anchor Beer is the best beer I've had since leaving Ireland. The gin you have is a bit rough, but it will do if you do as I show ya." Daniel put a block of ice in a canvas Lewis Bag and pounded it with a mallet until it was crushed into chips. He took six large long-stemmed martini glasses, coated the sides with the ice, and put them into the freezer. "Laddie, we have to wait a speck. 'Tis time to clean up the pub."

The men spent the next thirty minutes cleaning sawdust from the shelves and floor. Finally, Daniel said, "Laddie, fetch me your largest shaker."

John pulled an eighteen-inch tall silver shaker from under the bar and handed it to his pop.

"This will be the greatest martini ever made!"

"But Pop, we don't have any vermouth and the gin isn't very good."

Daniel continued on his mission without responding. He poured plenty of gin into the shaker with hunks of broken ice and shook it hard. John reached for the glasses in the freezer, and Daniel said, "Not yet, laddie." He took two toothpicks and put two olives and two miniature cocktail onions on each. Only after he shook the shaker again did Daniel go to the freezer and take out two glasses. The insides were coated with sparkling ice crystals. He put the olives and onions in each glass, shook the shaker hard one more time, and poured gin into the glasses. The crushed ice stayed frozen to the glass sides. The gin foamed with ice crystals from the shaker, like a snow cone. "Here's to Kelly's Bar," Daniel said, as he handed John a glass. They both took a drink.

"This is great, Pop. How did you know how to do it?"

"'Tis all show, Laddie. Make it look fancy and so cold nobody can taste the gin's bite. The ice will water down the drink so your customers won't get tipsy too fast. If it's for a lassie, you tell her you made it with love. Everyone will like it cause it 'tis the best."

John held up his glass and said, "It looks like a glass full of diamonds. That's what I call it, the Diamond Martini."

"'Tis a good enough name," Daniel said. "We will start the party tomorrow night at ten."

"But the law doesn't go into effect until midnight. What about the police?"

"Invite them, laddie. Have them bring their lassies and don't ever give them a tab. If you're gonna be a barkeep the paddies need to become your best friends."

"I don't know what I'd do without ya, Pop. I've never been in a real bar before."

"'Twas a shame when they passed Prohibition," Daniel said. "You laddies were deprived of the grand tradition of meeting your friends after work to wet your whistle while ya tell a few lies."

"We can charge twenty-one cents for your martinis, in honor of the Twenty-First Amendment."

After four more martinis, Daniel said, "Maybe you will find a pretty lassie here and you'll forget about that Jezebel."

"Pop," John said. "I don't ever want to talk about her again. I think I am done with women."

Nine o'clock Friday morning, John dragged himself out of bed and drank three glasses of water before making a pot of coffee. He poured two cups and knocked on Daniel's bedroom door. After thirty seconds, he opened the door as he said, "Get up, Pop. I got a cup of joe for ya." Daniel wasn't in his room. John's head was throbbing and spinning, and his nauseated stomach threatened to throw up any second. He had to focus on getting ready quickly to find Daniel and get the bar ready for tonight's grand opening. He arrived at ten fifteen to see his Pop standing atop a ladder over the entry. He was putting brass screws into a black mast over the entry. Hanging by brass chain links, a carved sign proclaimed in recessed Kelly green letters:

KELLY'S BAR
BEER 5¢
MARTINI 21¢

"Pop, the sign is beautiful!"

Daniel looked down and said, "Laddie, if you're to be a barkeep, 'tis high time ya learned how to drink."

Courtesy of Sunnyvale Historical Collection:
Murphy Avenue about 1930

"I think we shouldn't have had that last martini." John shielded the sun with his hand. "When did you make it?"

"'Twas five this morning I started carving it. Cedar, 'tis soft and chisels quickly. Ya need to keep it oiled or it will split."

December 4, 10:00 pm

That night, the bar was packed with men and women all dressed in suits and party dresses. There had been too few reasons for celebrating the last several years; Sunnyvale was ready to usher in the end of Prohibition properly.

"Good riddance to Prohibition!" Lou proclaimed to the entire bar as he lifted a glass of whiskey.

John wasn't sure how to react to Lou and Harold. What they had participated in revolted him, but it was in a moment of mass hysteria. Could he ever put it behind him? He didn't know and tonight wasn't the place to confront them and his own feelings.

Shouts of "Hear, hear!" and "I'll drink to that!" could be heard throughout the bar.

At five cents a pint, the beer flowed. John Kelly introduced himself to every customer. "I'm John Kelly, Irish and proud of it." He lifted his glass. "Here's to the start of better times. My pop built this bar and made the martinis."

John and Daniel couldn't make the martinis fast enough. A little after eleven, a tired-looking Brigitte Hernandez and her nineteen-year-old son, Ignacio, stepped up to the bar.

John noticed Ignacio's slender build and jet black hair. His black suit had shiny elbows and knees. The pants legs didn't cover his socks, and the arm cuffs were above his wrists.

"I'm John Kelly; welcome to my bar." John held out his hand.

Lou whispered to John, "That's Brigitte. This used to be her store."

John now remembered them at the bottom of the courthouse steps. He remembered Ignacio's intense eyes. He was a fine-looking young man.

John's face paled as he looked into Brigitte's eyes.

Brigitte said, "I'm glad you got the property instead of, pardon my French, that asshole Mr. Pierce. When I got sick, he came to me offering help. He only wanted to get ahold of the property. Besides, I got four hundred and three dollars because you bid over the loan amount."

"Well, I'm glad you got something out of it."

Brigitte put a nickel on the bar. "Am I going to die of thirst?"

"Your money will never be good in here," John said, as he poured Ignacio a beer and Brigitte a martini.

Ignacio looked at John. The bruises on his face had faded, but he still had two black eyes. He felt starstruck and thought how brave a man John was. "Thank you." He turned and said, "Mama, you need to sit."

John quickly turned to two inebriated gentlemen. "Give your seat to this wonderful woman." He ushered Ignacio and Brigitte to the barstools. He asked them how they were handling their situation. Ignacio said they were staying at the Sunnyvale Hotel across the street and he was looking for work. They had enough to last until then.

John said, "You come here tomorrow morning, I'll need help cleaning up this mess."

The next morning, Ignacio prepared thirty martini glasses with crushed ice and put them into the freezer just as John arrived. Ignacio grabbed the back of John's neck with his frozen hands.

"Jeez!" John pulled Ignacio's hands off, while laughing. "Damn, your hands are cold."

Ignacio reached for him again. "I got you good."

"Ha ha." John backed away with a big smile on his face. "We just got a delivery from Anchor. It's in the alley. We should bring it in before it grows legs."

Ignacio tilted a keg so John could slide the hand truck under it and roll it into the walk-in ice box. John said, "How's your mother doing?"

Ignacio tilted another keg. "Not well. She only leaves the room to use the bathroom in the hall. It is so sad; she was such a strong person."

"I am sure," John said. "When did she come here?"

"My parents fled Mexico during the Mexican Revolution. Poncho Villa was killing any French he found. My dad didn't think it was safe for my mom to stay. My dad died from the Spanish flu."

John said, "She had a hard life. Does she still have enough money to stay at the hotel?"

Ignacio just shrugged his shoulders. "She has the four hundred dollars from the sale."

John pulled three silver dollars from the drawer under the counter and handed them to him. "Thanks, and I will see you tomorrow."

★★★

That evening, Peter Neil slapped his empty mug on the bar and slurred, "Hey, John, I'll have another."

John could see something was bothering him; he wasn't making any jokes and he guzzled his beer. John refilled the mug. "How's the world treating you, Peter?"

"Oh, just peachy," He put a nickel on the bar. "Except I've been out of work for two months. I can't pay my mortgage; the bank already sent me a notice."

John pushed the nickel back. "This one is on the house."

"Thank you, John, but that won't keep a roof over my family." Peter downed the beer John had just poured him. "I should burn the house down just to keep that fuckin' banker from getting it."

"Mr. Pierce?" John asked.

"That's the fucker. He's not a friend of yours, is he?"

John had never seen Peter making a scene before. He poured himself an Anchor beer. "No, I just know how he operates. Let's go sit down in the back."

John brought Peter to the back booth and they both took a drink of beer. "Would you be interested in a job in San Francisco?"

Peter set his mug down and looked at John with a stupid grin on his face. "What do you mean?"

"My pop keeps trying to get me to go back to San Francisco and he said he can get me a job building the bridge across The Golden Gate. I am sure he would do the same for you if I asked him."

Peter gaped at him. "Holy shit, really?"

John said. "I'll call him tonight, but I know he will do it."

"Are you sure about this?" Peter said. "I have been looking for work for months."

"I'll get my pop to check tomorrow. You'll get the job." John emptied his mug. "About your house; you can't burn it down. You'll end up in jail, and what if someone is hurt?"

Peter shook his head. "I know, but I just don't want fuckin' banker Pierce to get my home."

"How much do you owe the bank?" John asked

"About two hundred and fifty dollars. Why?"

John said, "I've been so busy starting the bar I haven't had time to buy a house. I'm staying at Mrs. Jones's boarding house. I'll buy it from you; we can meet at the bank tomorrow and sign the papers in front of Mr. Pierce."

Three days passed. Ignacio was doing the morning preparations. John didn't arrive until after eleven o'clock. "Good morning, Ignacio; everything looks good."

"Thank you," Ignacio said.

John flipped a key that Ignacio snatched out of the air. "What's this?"

"I just bought Peter's house on McKinley Street. I want you to clean it up for me."

Ignacio scratched his head. He would be willing to help him with anything, "Sure, I am happy to."

"It has three bedrooms and a large porch." John walked behind the bar and poured a beer for each of them. He came around and sat on a stool next to Ignacio and slowly lifted his mug. "Here's to our new home."

Ignacio set his mug down. "I don't understand."

"You and Brigitte will move in today. I don't want you at that flea bag any longer."

Ignacio's face lit up with a huge smile and tears ran down his cheeks. "John, are you sure?"

"Yes, I'm sure. Your mother needs a better place."

July 1934

Brigitte's funeral was at St. Martin's Church. Every pew and aisle was packed with perspiring mourners. John sat next to Ignacio in the front. The priest gave the eulogy and said, "John Kelly has invited everyone back to his bar for an old-fashioned Irish wake." The irony of Brigitte being French and Ignacio half-Mexican wasn't lost on anyone at the mass.

The bar had not been this full since its opening party. Sunnyvale was having an unusual heat wave. It was over one hundred degrees and the packed bar became humid even with the front and back doors open. Suit jackets and ties were stacked on a booth in the back. John provided an open bar and the locals brought six potato salads, sliced roast beef, bread, pies, cakes, and every wife's favorite company dish.

Officer Pat O'Riley wore his dress blue uniform. "John, 'tis a nice thing you are doing today. I will stick around and help you with anyone who has a few too many."

"Well, Pat," John said, taking off his tie, "you may be needing to take me home before long."

John stood on top of the bar. "Thank you all for coming," he said. "I have only known Brigitte for these last few months, but she was a wonderful woman and I raise a glass in her honor."

Many people stood up to attest to how wonderful Brigitte was.

Ignacio was in tears as John hugged him. John had tears rolling down his cheek as well. "Now, lad," he said. "You are not alone. Look at how this entire town is out here just to let you know you are loved."

John closed the bar down at two a.m. He helped Ignacio walk back to the house, as he was very unsteady after an evening of drinking. It was still hot and humid at the house, so John opened all the windows. He stripped to his boxer shorts, as did Ignacio. They sat and talked, and Ignacio cried over the loss of his mother.

John stood and hugged Ignacio to comfort him. Their sweaty bodies slid against each other. Ignacio felt the tingle of John's fingers as he slid his hand down his back. Ignacio pushed closer as John's touch stimulated him.

"She was a great woman, and you will always miss her." John felt Ignacio's penis slowly becoming erect. It pressed against his leg. The sweaty boxers only made his penis feel uncovered against John's sweaty leg. Ignacio was not making any effort to move it.

John was surprised when he felt his own penis getting hard.

He thought to himself, God forgive me as I am committing a mortal sin.

They woke up in the morning in the same bed, contentedly embracing each other.

CHAPTER 9

August 21, 2000

That evening, Mary was sitting on the couch, chewing the edge of her fingernail while reading a paperback copy of *Angela's Ashes*. Johnny was in bed and Bill was still at work. She was dreading going to work at Space Key because of her asshole boss, Edmond, who constantly hit on her. She felt like a slave there; she needed an escape and cherished having a quiet house and being lost in a great, moving novel. As she turned the page with her finger, a drop of blood from her chewed cuticle dripped onto the page. She licked her finger and wiped the spot, but it only spread the stain more. She re-read a line of chapter seventeen twice. Mary sucked her finger in an attempt to ease the sting of the torn cuticle. She read, "Frank slaps his girl-friend Angela in the face and accuses her of infidelity." Suddenly, she was unable to stop an oncoming panic attack. Mary had succeeded in repressing her childhood memories, but now she pulled her knees to her chest as she felt the emotions of her own childhood trauma come back.

Mary's mother Aislin was in the kitchen preparing dinner. Mary was at the table, practicing her eighth-grade spelling words aloud. Aislin whispered, "Please be quiet doing your homework. Your father is watching the game."

The A's and the Dodgers were playing the first game of the 1988 World Series. Kieran seemed happy as the A's were ahead. He yelled at the screen after almost every pitch. It was now the bottom of the ninth inning, and the A's ace closer Dennis Eckersley was only one pitch away from winning the game. Kirk Gibson, the most valuable player in 1988, had injured both legs a couple of days earlier. Surprisingly, he hobbled in as a pinch hitter with two outs. He could barely walk. This was a desperate move by the Dodgers. Eckersley got two quick called strikes. Kieran took a swallow of Colt .45 malt, stood up in anticipation of the last pitch and said, "One hundred is in the bank."

Eckersley threw three more pitches, two balls and one hit foul; the count was 2 and 2. Davis, the tying run, stole second base. Kieran stepped closer to the TV. "Come on; one more strike!"

Eckersley set into the stretch, wound up and pitched a fastball. Gibson swung hard and hit a home run. He hobbled around the bases and was nearly injured by his own players, who just wanted to hug him for winning the game. In an instant, Kieran yelled, "Fuck!" He walked into the kitchen, empty Colt .45 bottle still in hand, and opened a cabinet. "Fuck, did you take my whiskey?"

Aislin trembled. "You finished it last night."

"Bullshit," Kieran, a red-headed Scotsman, growled, his blue veins showing through his pale skin. He tossed the bottle aimlessly across the kitchen, hitting Aislin in the lip.

Mary quickly handed Aislin a dishtowel for the blood pouring on her dress. Kieran ordered her mother to get him another beer.

Mary jumped up. "I'll get it." Her heart was pounding.

Kieran grabbed her by the hair, slammed her against the refrigerator, and surrounded her face with his right hand, pinning Mary. She could smell the beer and cigar smoke on Kieran and his eyes were void of any humanity. Aislin got up and grabbed Kieran around his waist and tried to pull him off Mary. Without turning his face, Kieran backhanded a wild blow to Aislin, smashing her left ear, almost knocking her out.

Mary's body trembled and her sweat-dampened cotton blouse clung to her. "You think you're grown up now that you got boobs," Kieran grunted, continuing to push his right palm into Mary's face while holding her defensively against the refrigerator. He squeezed her face until Mary screamed in agony. "Don't you ever talk back to me again, you little whore!" Kieran slammed Mary into the corner of the refrigerator, cracking her cheek bone as blood poured out of her mouth.

Kieran looked back at Mary and Aislin, both on the floor, blood flowing from their faces. He grabbed his coat and walked out the door. Mary stayed cowering in the corner on the floor, afraid to move, holding a napkin to her mouth.

Angela's Ashes laid on the floor as Mary sat in the fetal position on the couch, knees still pulled tightly against her chest. Her wet body was now cold. She shivered and her right arm trembled out of control, flying over her head.

Bill arrived at home at about 2:20 in the morning with Hippie Paul's laptop under his arm. Mary lifted her head, still covered in sweat. "Are you h-hungry, dear?" she stuttered. "I cooked steak and French fries. I'll heat them up for you." Mary couldn't stop stuttering and her arm still trembled. Bill never understood or had patience when she would be overwhelmed by anxiety attacks and tremors. He had no concept of how anyone couldn't control their emotions.

"No, don't bother yourself. I pigged out on a pizza at work."

Mary was relieved and sat on the couch, taking deep breaths for fifteen minutes. Her arms loosened as her body calmed down. Bill couldn't deal with her attacks, so he just ignored them until they subsided. Arguing usually was a hot button that set off her anxiety. She couldn't handle Bill's aggressiveness when she criticized him. It would trigger her stuttering and tremors as well. Worse yet, when they had an argument and she started to stutter, Bill would just say, "Not again." And he would walk away as if she weren't fighting fair.

However, if she became pissed off enough, her anger would override her inner timidity. Today, she was protecting her son. "Did you put the exploding snakes into Johnny's lunch today?" Mary's heart was still racing, but she was mad, not overcome by anxiety.

"Yeah, did he get scared?"

"It isn't funny." Mary looked into Bill's eyes. "Mrs. Laddy, of all people, opened it and everyone around dropped their lunches. Johnny had to clean up the mess and spent the rest of the day in the principal's office. He is very upset and doesn't want to go to school tomorrow."

Bill interrupted. "Those stupid people don't have a sense of humor. I can't believe they're upset. It was a good joke; I only wish I could have been there to see it."

Mary raised her voice. "Damn it. Don't interrupt me. Johnny is shy and he was yelled at and is in trouble because you wanted to make a joke. Well, it is only funny to you!"

"Sorry." Bill set the computer on the coffee table. "I won't do it again."

Mary picked her book up off the floor and set it on the table. "Whose computer is that?"

"It's mine," Bill answered.

"Where did you get it?" Mary walked over to the table, looking at the laptop, and opened it up. "This is a great laptop. It's an Apple PowerBook. This is really expensive."

"Why don't you mind your own damn business?" Bill said.

Mary twisted her finger in her hair while looking at the Apple on her lap. She slid her hand down the smooth, sleek case. She lifted it and was surprised by how light it was.

"If you must know, Miss Busybody, someone left it at the bar. I figured I could sell it for a few bucks," Bill said as he walked to the refrigerator to get a beer. He opened the door and looked inside to find a full six-pack of Beck's and two cartons of eggs. He grabbed a beer with his left hand, took a BIC[a] lighter out of his pocket and used it to pry off the bottle cap.

"Nobody's going to forget a computer and not come back for it." Mary tapped her finger. "He's going to complain to the police if you sell it."

"I'm not worried about him coming back." Bill stopped for a long drink of the Beck's, sat down at the kitchen table, and turned a page of the paper. "Thanks for getting eggs."

"Eggs!" Mary said. "Don't talk about the eggs. Why isn't he coming back?"

"He died at the bar tonight," Bill answered.

"My stars! That's awful!" Mary pushed the laptop away and looked up at Bill nervously. "Did you know him?"

"Not really," said Bill. "Paul was the hermit I told you about. He came in every day. He never talked to anyone. He just sat in a booth and typed on this stupid computer. He was a bum; I doubt anyone will ever miss him."

"That's so sad. You should see if he has any family," Mary said.

"Don't be a sap," Bill continued. "I took the guy's computer. I'm not going to go near his family if he has any. I'll sell the computer at the pawn shop on my way to work."

Mary put the laptop back on the coffee table. "How's your beer?"

"I could go for another." Bill took another drink from the half-empty beer bottle.

"How much will you get for it?" Mary asked, as she opened another Beck's.

"I don't know; a hundred bucks or so. Who cares; it didn't cost me anything."

"Don't sell it." Mary had difficulty getting her words out. "We'll never be able to afford a good computer. This thing cost a couple grand. Let me have it. I will make good use of it and you will always be able to sell it later."

Bill shrugged, "I don't care. If you want it, take it."

"Oh, thank you! This is really great."

Mary sat down with the laptop and started to check out the programs, experimenting with the graphics. Her hand was still shaking and made it difficult to use the keyboard.

Bill looked at her. "Don't fall in love with it. It is just another toy; you'll get tired of it."

Mary pondered whether or not to tell Bill to eat shit and die, but said, "Thank you, dear. Do you want some chips and salsa to go with your beer?"

"Yeah, sure."

Bill picked up his second beer and turned on the TV. All the networks had the primary election coverage.

"I hate all this shit. Who cares about who's winning school board seats? It doesn't matter anymore; Bush and Kerry won the nominations weeks before we ever got to vote. Why don't the networks draw straws and only the loser has to show the election results?" Bill channel surfed until he found *American Graffiti* on channel 36. "Hey, Mary, the best damn movie ever made is on."

Mary looked up from the computer screen. "How many times have you watched that movie?"

"You just don't get it; this is a classic. This is what I used to do on Friday nights," Bill said as he finished his second beer.

Bill turned on the surround sound and turned up the volume. Wolfman Jack and 1960s music filled the house. He lay back on the couch and drank another beer. Mary found new energy and continued playing with the laptop into the early morning hours. She explored the different files in the computer and was surprised to find one labeled "Third Draft." She opened it and spent the rest of the night engrossed. Her body was finally calm.

CHAPTER 10

Johnny lay awake in his bed; he hadn't slept much while worrying about school. The morning sunlight lit up the pull-down shade like the Capital Drive-in's projection screen between films. He loved it when his parents took him to the drive-in theater, although he usually fell asleep halfway through the movie.

Johnny was terrified that Mrs. Laddy and the principal would continue to punish him for the commotion he caused with the can of joke snakes. If I climb up on the roof and pretend I am still sleeping, nobody would want to wake me. They would be afraid that I would fall. Nah! That won't work. I will have to wake up sometime.

He considered slamming his door shut with his fingers in the door jam. It would hurt, but I broke my finger before and it wasn't that bad. I spent the rest of the day at the doctor's, getting a cast on my hand. The bedroom door won't work. It's not heavy and closes easily. No, I'll use the front door. It is so heavy I have to slam it shut all the time. Mom and Dad would believe it was an accident. He devised the plan. If I leave my lunch on the counter and remember it just before Dad closes the door, I could run back in, grab the lunch pail, run out and slam the door. It would be so fast that it might not even hurt that much.

In the living room, Mary was still on the couch, wrapped in a blanket with the laptop lying on its side on the floor.

Bill woke up alone in the bedroom and stared at the clock. Mary wasn't in bed. "Mary, where the fuck are you?" Bill sprang up and went into the living room to see Mary struggling to open her eyes. "It's seven-forty-five." Bill shook Mary until she appeared coherent. "Johnny will be late for school and you'll get yourself fired. Get your ass up now!"

Mary's heart raced; she couldn't be late again. But she needed to tell Bill: "Paul was a great writer and wrote a fantastic novel."

"What the hell are you talking about?" Bill pulled Mary's arm up and got her on her feet. "He was a crackpot, a bum."

"No, really! The novel on the computer is good. You have to read it. I couldn't put it down."

"What is it about?"

"It's a spy novel that takes place at Space Key. He must have worked there because he describes exactly what a shitty company it is to work for. Anyway, Xing Juan Zhang is a spy for the Chinese. She steals our top-secret technology from Space Key to sell to the Chinese army. She returns to Hong Kong and she and her mother are murdered for the disc."

Bill sat on the arm of the couch. "Is it worth anything?"

"Well, yeah, if you could sell it. I mean if you aren't a marketable author already, you will never get someone to read it, let alone buy it."

"That doesn't make any sense. How would we ever get new authors?"

"Only one in a hundred, no, make that one in a thousand, new authors ever get published. Well, except for tell-all gossip books. You could spend years trying to get anyone who counts just to read this. Besides, you didn't write it."

"You get your ass off the couch; we need to get moving. I'll take a look at it after we get Johnny to school."

Johnny sat up and carefully listened to the yelling. This might be his big chance. Everyone was late, so maybe they would just let him stay home if he said he was sick. Johnny tossed the blanket back over his head and rubbed his hand on his forehead as fast and hard as he could. The friction started to hurt but it might work. When he heard his mother in the hall he put his head on the pillow and pretended to be asleep.

Mary quietly opened the bedroom door, walked in, and sat sideways on the edge of the bed. She slid the palm of her hand across Johnny's forehead and through his hair, "Johnny, it's time to get up. It's a beautiful sunny day."

Johnny put his hands on his stomach, moaned, and said, "Mom, I feel sick. I feel like I am going to throw up."

Mary put her hand back onto his forehead and said, "You do feel a little warm."

"Can I stay home from school today?" Johnny asked. "Oh, my stomach really, really hurts." Johnny crossed both arms tightly across his stomach and groaned again.

Mary stood up walked toward the door. "I'm going to go get the thermometer."

Johnny quickly looked around the room for anything to help him. He sat up, reached atop the nightstand, and pulled the chain on his lamp. When Mary returned to the room she stood next to Johnny, placed her hand on his forehead again. It didn't feel as warm this time.

"Here, keep this under your tongue until I get back." Mary said as she put the thermometer into his mouth. As soon as Mary left the room, Johnny took the thermometer and placed the silver tip directly on the warm light bulb and held it there until he heard Bill's footsteps. Johnny put it back into his mouth and resumed his position of holding his stomach.

Bill walked in and looked at his son curled up and moaning and said, "What a faker."

He reached down and took out the thermometer and yelled, "Mary, you better call 911! Johnny has a fever of one hundred and ten!"

Bill put his hand on Johnny's cool forehead, "I think I better throw you into the bathtub filled with ice water before your brain is fried."

"Come on, Dad." Johnny groaned. "I really feel sick. My stomach hurts."

Bill grabbed the blankets and pulled them off Johnny. "Come on; get your butt out of bed. We're already late. It was a good try, but I'm not buying it." As Bill walked out of the room, he yelled back, "And if you aren't dressed in the kitchen in two minutes, I'll give you a what-for!"

Johnny held his stomach. "What's a what-for?"

Bill looked back. "When I slap you on your ass, you're going to ask me *WHAT FOR?*"

Bill quickly made French toast. Mary poured two cups of coffee, handed Bill his cup, and said, "You know why he doesn't want to go to school, don't you?"

"Ah, come on, Mary. The school is making a big deal about nothing. It was funny." Bill turned toward the bedrooms and yelled to Johnny, "You got five seconds left. You better be out here." Bill took the French toast off the grill and while putting it onto three plates yelled, "One... Twoooooooooooooo... Threeeeeeeeeeeeeeeeeeeee."

Johnny stumbled into the kitchen, tucking his shirt into his pants while trying to squirm his feet into his tennis shoes. He reached down and used his finger to shoehorn his heel into the shoes. Mary placed her hand on his cool forehead again. Johnny grabbed his stomach and said, "Mom, my stomach really does hurt."

Bill put the plate of French toast on the kitchen table and said, "Here, eat your breakfast; you'll feel better. Get yourself something to drink."

Johnny opened the refrigerator and grabbed the carton of orange juice, then took a glass off the counter and half-filled it. He sat down at the table and started pushing his fork between the pieces of French toast. Bill quickly ate his toast as he started making Johnny's lunch. When Bill left the room, Johnny scooped the French toast into his napkin and took a drink of his orange juice. He opened the refrigerator door and filled the rest of his glass with diet Coke from an opened two-liter bottle. Johnny ran down the hall, stomping his feet and making a groaning Ahhhhhhhh noise. When he reached the toilet bowl, he dumped the French toast from the napkin into the bowl and then dumped the Coke and orange juice from his glass. Johnny threw himself over the bowl. "Yuuuuahhhhhhhhhh. I threw up," he yelled to his parents.

Bill and Mary both walked down the hall toward the bathroom. Bill stepped in front of Mary to see first. Johnny held the toilet with a drunkard's grip. "I threw up. I told you I was sick."

Bill put his hand on Johnny's forehead, lifted his head from over the toilet, and grabbed Johnny's hand before he could reach the flusher. Bill leaned over to carefully inspect the vomit and remarked, "That French toast came out of you in good enough condition that I could put it right back on your plate."

Bill turned his face to Johnny, then back to look into the bowl.

"I don't even see any bite marks. Look, that piece still has syrup on it. That orange juice was a good touch, but I can't tell what you put in there to make it dark."

Bill looked up at Mary and said, "Mary, doesn't that still look good enough to eat?"

He turned to Johnny and said, "Do you think I'm stupid? I've invented every trick in the book on how to get out of going to school. You need to learn how to make better puke. The French toast might have worked if you chewed it up first."

Bill released the grip he had on Johnny's flushing hand and put his arm on his shoulder, "The way I used to do it, I would chew my food extra mushy before spiting in into a napkin. Then when I threw it into the bowl, it would float out evenly across the water surface. Just like real puke."

Johnny shook his head.

Bill said, "I heard old Mrs. Laddy got scared by your snakes."

Johnny said, "Come on, Dad. I got in trouble. Now everyone hates me."

Bill hesitated. "I'm sorry you got in trouble, but it was a good joke. How could I know she was going to open it. What did she do?"

Johnny lifted his head to look directly at Bill. "She called me a brat and said DAMN."

Bill strained trying to keep a straight face. "Now stop being silly and brush your teeth so we can get you to school."

Bill and Mary returned to the bedroom. Bill said, "That kid will be a pretty good con man one day. Although that French toast was awful bad; it was almost whole."

Mary turned her head to keep Bill from seeing her smile. "I still don't think it was funny. Do you want the car today?"

"Yeah," Bill said, "I want to see what I can do with our book. Hurry up and I'll drop you off."

Johnny slowly brushed his teeth and hair. When Bill called him to leave, he ran to the front door, right past his lunch box on the kitchen table, and caught up to Bill at the front door. He waited until the door was opened and they both were outside. Johnny turned around and said, "Oh, I forgot my lunch."

Just as he started running back through the door, Mary was there to meet them with his lunch pail. A very disappointed Johnny said, "Oh, thanks, Mom."

Bill, Mary, and Johnny walked to the driveway. Bill pulled the car cover off his 1968 Chevrolet El Camino. He stood back to admire it. When he bought the car ten years earlier for a bargain price of one thousand dollars, the interior seats were torn, the engine smoked, and the body was rusted and dented. Bill had the seats recovered, rebuilt the engine himself, and finally, only one year ago, sprang for Maaco's $300 Presidential paint job. The red paint started to oxidize after six months, so Bill bought a $150 custom car cover. Bill opened the right-side passenger door with his key and had Johnny slide across the seat to unlock the driver's door. The key no longer worked on his door. The door opened with a large creaking sound, then Bill got in and slammed the door twice before it latched shut. Mary slid into the right side, leaving Johnny in the middle.

"I'm squished. I hate this truck. Mike and Don make fun of me every time they see me get out of it. They also hit me all the time."

"This is a classic!" Bill said, "I don't know why anyone would want a new car when you can have a great ride like this. I will make you a deal. You go to school and I will teach you how to box. In the back of Kelly's, I have a speed bag. OK? It will be fun."

"OK, Dad."Bill drove up to the corner across from the school. Mary opened the door, making room for Johnny to get out. Johnny got out and looked for a slow-moving car he could throw himself into. The crossing guard came out to protect the crosswalk, wrecking his plan. Bill said, "You have fun at school today, and I don't want to get a call from school claiming you're sick; got it?"

Johnny looked back. "Yeah... all right." Johnny walked through the cyclone fence gate onto the asphalted school yard.

Jason, Assad, and Kimberley ran up to him. Jason said, "Hey Johnny, that was really funny yesterday. You got Mrs. Laddy really good. She even went home crying."

Assad squeezed through the kids to see Johnny's face. "She even said damn."

Six more children came running. All Johnny could hear were voices, all talking over each other.

"That was a great joke, Johnny."

"How did you get Mrs. Laddy to open it?"

"That was really cool."

Soon, all the children in the schoolyard were gathered around. Mike said, "That was the best joke I've ever seen. You sure got a lot of guts. How did you make it?"

Johnny was surrounded. He stood there, listening to a hundred questions. Finally he said, "I took the snakes out of a joke can-of-nuts and put them into a Tupperware. I knew it would scare her."

Don patted Johnny on the back, and rubbed his hand through his hair.

Johnny said, "Did you see the food all over her?"

"Hey, Johnny, do you want to be on my kickball team today?" Mike asked.

"Yeah, maybe," Johnny said.

The bell rang and the mob of students ran toward their classrooms. When Johnny got to the door, Jason, Don, and Liz made space for him to cut into the line.

★★★

Bill walked through the aisle flanked with copiers toward the Kinko's counter. Two employees were working at the registers. A middle-aged man with a ridiculous comb-over was at one register finishing a sale. Bill stared at a young woman as she assisted a customer with an order for business cards. Her blond hair was very short, spiked with gel and highlighted with purple tips. He waited about five minutes until she was done with her customer, then rushed up with the Apple computer in hand.

"May I help you?" The nametag on her pink tank top read Irene.

"How's your day going?"

"Shitty. This was supposed to be my day off."

"Irene, that's my little sister's name," Bill said. "You look like her, too. You're both beautiful."

Irene blushed, looking away to compose herself. "Yeah, right. Is there something I can help you with?"

"Oh, I'm sorry. I didn't mean to embarrass you, but you do look exactly like my sister."

Irene rolled her hazel eyes. "I'm not embarrassed!"

Bill said, "I wrote a novel and I want to print it out."

"You must be thrilled to have finished it. How many pages is it?"

"I think it is about 325 pages. Why?" Bill stared into her hazel eyes with hopes of sweeping her off her feet.

Irene pulled out four sample bindings from under the counter and spread them out on the counter.

"Well, I could just print out a copy, but I think you should let me bind it for you, if you want copies to read or to give out. Have you looked at our binding options?"

"No, I haven't."

"I can bookbind it for you with a cloth tape and soft cover, or you might want it bound with a spiral wire. This will allow you to lay it flat as you read it. I can show you." She rolled her eyes. Why doesn't he just pick one?

"I like this one." Bill held up a spiral-bound pamphlet with a colorful blue plastic cover. "How much would it cost for ten copies?"

She got out an order pad, worked on the calculations, and said, "$252.00 plus tax. If you are send-

ing it to publishers, you will also need unbound dou-
ble-spaced copies with the pages numbered. They
won't look at anything that isn't formatted properly; it
needs to be on twenty-pound paper and only printed
on one side."

"You seem to know a lot about this. How about
six copies bound and six copies prepared to send out."

"I can do that."

"OK, do it that way. When will it be ready?" Bill
placed the laptop on the counter and turned it toward
Irene.

"I never had anyone ever bring in his whole computer." Irene shook her head as she clicked some keys
on the laptop. "Next time you only need to bring in a
copy on a disc. Do you want to buy a disc so I can copy
it and you can take your computer with you?"

"Yes, sure. That will help me a lot."

Irene looked down the entire time she copied
the file onto the disc from the computer. As if anyone
would read this, she thought. She copied the novel onto
a disk and printed an invoice, avoiding eye contact. "It
will be ready for you tomorrow morning. Anyone in
the store can finish the sale for you."

Bill signed the invoice. "How about if I pick it
up at noon and take you out for lunch? You seem to
know a lot about getting published. I think you could
help me."

"I don't think so. I may be off tomorrow," Irene
groaned.

CHAPTER 11

The Printed Circuit Board Assembly Room was depressingly drab with a suspended ceiling, fluorescent lights, dark gray carpet, and light gray cubicles. There were no windows or outside light apart from a few yellowed and weathered fiberglass skylights in the suspended ceiling. The East Sunnyvale Campus of Space Key occupied fifty acres. Mary and Dawn worked under Edmond Garcia in the electronics quality control building for prototype production. They had shared their feelings, thoughts, and life's problems for five years. Dawn, thirty-six and slightly overweight, with brown shoulder-length hair and dressed in a bright orange blouse and black pants, had been divorced two years ago while she was pregnant with her second son. Jack, her husband of ten years, left her for a twenty-year-old blond named Christy.

When Dawn was bored, she would tease Mary. "Hey, Mary, why don't you install a picture of a big Jamaican dick on your computer as the screensaver?"

"Damn it," Mary, red-faced, would whisper back, "You don't have to be so loud. Edmond might hear you. Don't you have an inside voice?"

"No, I don't, and I don't care if Edmond hears me. I hope he fires me so I can get unemployment, that asshole."

Mary rolled her eyes and kept her head down so Dawn couldn't see her smile. "Are big dicks the only thing you ever think about?"

Dawn loudly said, "Is there anything else better to think about?"

"Well, I guess if you haven't seen one for," Mary paused, "what's it been, two years since you've had one?"

"Believe me, it's been an eternity."

"That's what you need," Mary said.

"Right now, I wouldn't be choosey. I will take any man."

Mary stuttered, "Well at least you have an excuse. I can't remember the last time either. Bill's been such an asshole, drinking too much, throwing temper tantrums, and being mean to Johnny."

Dawn said, "I can't believe he would be mean to Johnny."

Mary told her about the snakes in his lunch and how Johnny was sent to the principal's office and tried everything to get out of going to school.

Dawn started to giggle. "Bill didn't mean for Johnny to get into trouble. Shit, it really was kind of funny."

"What! You're taking his side?"

"Well, no, I meant that he is just trying to do special things for Johnny, in his own way. It's the same reason a little boy will give a frog to a little girl he has a crush on. I think he was just trying to be nice."

"Well, maybe you know me too well. He did give me a computer last night."

"What? Your cheap, penny-pinching, still-drives-the-same-beat-to-shit-El Camino-he-bought-ten-years-ago husband, bought you a computer? What is it? An old IBM 386?" Dawn got out of her chair and walked around the partition to hear the story.

Mary looked up. "No, it's an Apple PowerBook." She paused. "With the 17-inch screen, no less."

"What?" Dawn said, "I can't believe he bought it."

"Well, I never said he bought it. He got it from work."

Dawn put her hands on her hips. "Since when do they give out computers at bars? Oh, let me guess, there was a stack of them next to the pretzels and he just took one."

"You're such a comedian." Mary crossed her hands on her chest. "Someone left it in the bar."

"So what happens when they come back?" Dawn asked.

Mary sat still, staring at her for almost a minute. "I guess we will have to give it back."

"Mary, don't be stupid! This is the same man who, when you found someone else's credit card in his wallet, claimed, 'Oh, the waiter last night must have gotten the cards mixed up.' There's gotta be more to it than what he is telling you."

"I know he screws up sometimes, but I think I can trust him this time."

Dawn walked back to her station and sat down. "Well, I hope I don't have to bail you out of jail." She started to work on a circuit board, stopped, and added, "That Apple is really good for graphics. I bet you could make your own stationery with the Jamaican dick on it."

Mary looked up just in time to see Edmond in his tan suit with a turtleneck shirt. "Shush! He's coming toward us."

Edmond said to Dawn as he walked by, not even making eye contact, "Make sure you flux the contact before you solder the capacitor to the board."

He rounded the cubicle and leaned over Mary, putting his arm on her shoulder, and said, while looking down her cleavage, "Great job, Mary. I want to take you out for lunch to discuss your future here at Space Key."

Mary started to shake. "Not now," she stuttered.

Edmond drew his hand off her shoulder, sliding it across her neck, and ran his fingers through her red hair. "OK, maybe next week."

As he turned and walked away, Mary's arm uncontrollably flung above her head. She felt sick to her stomach and began hyperventilating. Dawn had seen Mary have panic attacks before but never when she was this much out of control. She got up and helped Mary to the parking lot before anyone else saw her. "Take some deep breaths; it will help." They sat down on a bench in the courtyard. "Do you want me to call Bill to come and get you?"

"No, I just need to zone out for a while. If I think about something else, it will pass. That asshole practically molested me." Mary pulled a prescription bottle of Valium from her purse and swallowed two pills.

Dawn held Mary. "He's an asshole and enjoys coming on to good-looking women. You notice he didn't give me the time of day. You should consider yourself lucky that you are still a beautiful woman."

Mary was trembling and stuttering so much that it took forever to get the words out. "I wish I was ugly and men never looked at me."

"Try to calm down, Mary; don't think about him. If men freak you out, why are you OK with Bill?"

"Bill and I share a lot of issues in common. Besides, he was my knight in shining armor."

Dawn took her arm off Mary and looked her in the face. "Bill! A knight in shining armor?"

Mary was in no condition to explain.

"Nevertheless, you need to concentrate on something positive. Think about Johnny doing everything he could to get out of school. That fake puke you told me about was pretty funny."

It took about forty-five minutes for the Valium and Dawn to get Mary calmed down.

"Tell me how Bill was your knight in armor?"

Mary said, "He saved me from an asshole. We need to get back to work." They only had an hour of work left and it went by quickly.

CHAPTER 12

Rodger's cubicle at Space Key was stacked high with legal-sized folders. Colorful Post-it® notes were attached everywhere: on files, the edges of the flat-screen monitor, even the calendar, which hung by a straightened-out paper clip, and which had so many Post-its® on it that you couldn't read it. A half-dozen charts and graphs hung next to a Post-it®-covered framed photograph of Herman Wiseman. A half-empty Starbucks coffee cup with white mold floating in it had a Post-it® note with the formula $sin -\frac{2}{3}\sqrt{2^n} \geq \frac{1}{2} E + 2X^2 - 1$written on it and stuck on the handle. Even the Gold Plate Award proclaiming RODGER HINDS - SPACE-KEY 1999 EMPLOYEE OF THE YEAR, had three Post-it® notes hanging on it. A gold-framed picture of a young Asian women inscribed with *"RIP Xing Juan Zhang"* stood out as it was the only item not covered with Post-it® notes. The top of a clear straw protruding from a large Coke cup was indented with teeth marks. A half-eaten burger lay on its yellow wrapper surrounded by droplets of grease, mustard, and catsup.

Rodger clicked the mouse to open his next e-mail and took another bite from the burger. A little juice leaked out of the corner of his mouth. He wiped it with his finger then sucked his finger clean. A Snickers candy bar wrapper was wadded up next to the remains of a Krispy Kreme glazed donut. The garbage can was overflowing with computer printouts, a book of magic rested against the monitor, and a two-inch tall voodoo doll was hanging from the tan fabric divider by a stick-pin through its head.

Rodger read an e-mail from Steven Case, president of technology development:

Rodger,

Thank you for your input. I appreciate the fact that you value your work and are dedicated to making Space Key's product better; however, I personally recalculated all the equations and could not duplicate the problems or locate the virus you claim exists. Your assertion that the Chinese government is hacking our software is bordering on paranoia. You are an important member of the team who developed this new technology. The Navy is excited to have this new submarine detection equipment. If you continue to make these accusations, I will need to begin disciplinary actions.

Thank you,
Steven Case

Rodger's short fingers danced across the keyboard in reply to the e-mail. He paused to push up the nose-piece of his black horn-rimmed glasses and grabbed his Kernighan and Ritchie programming guide. As he studied the book index, he continued to reposition his glasses. Ever since he sat on the glasses last month and bent the right hinge, they continuously would slip down his nose. Rodger found the proper specification and typed two pages, ending the response with:

> I repeated my test 4 times before sending you my observation. Each time the error occurred and I could see evidence of a virus. Suddenly after I voice my concern I can no longer make the error appear using the same prompt. Obviously we have a cover-up.

He added four recipients as "Cc" to the message and clicked SEND.

Peggy, a programmer, looked over the messy desk, took a half-step back, and said, "We have pizza in the break room for finishing the project you created. Come join the party."

Rodger pushed the last bite of the hamburger into his mouth. This time, part of the bun dropped, hitting his pencil protector and landing on the floor. The shirttail was out from his pants in the rear, exposing a roll of white skin and the waistband of Christmas-tree print boxer shorts. "I already ate, and there's something funny going on. I used to run this department; software couldn't be released until I said so! Since Steven Case took over the management, nobody cares. There is something wrong with the stealth sub software and there is a cover-up. I know, because I developed it, and I think the program was intentionally sabotaged."

"You think Steven has something to do with the problem?"

"Yes, I do! Steven is going to pay a price, that asshole."

Rodger looked up at Peggy and said, "I just can't work today; I'm too stressed."

Peggy thought, He has been psycho ever since ever since Xing Juan was murdered. She put her index finger under his chin and gently lifted his face to look at her. "You need a vacation." She turned her eyes to the photo and asked, "Is that your father?"

"No. Herman Wiseman, he was like a father to me. He hired me to help him at his toy and magic store when I was twelve. He was getting too old to move boxes and put away inventory. His two sons, Harvey and Stan, were lowlife druggies who thought they were too good to work in his store. Herman always encouraged me to pursue my education and had faith that I could become a good engineer. I rearranged his entire store to maximize the space. I made room to hold twenty-five percent more stock. I even helped him with his groceries and house chores. I was a latch-key kid from a poor family, but Herman would always feed me and give me extra money for movies or books. I got accepted to Cal Berkeley, but I couldn't afford it! Herman told me that he would make sure my tuition was paid. Two weeks before high school graduation, he died, and I lost the only person who ever took an interest in me."

Peggy interrupted, "The pizza is going to get cold."

Rodger just ignored her. "He didn't have much of value except the collectibles and inventory in his store. His kids figured that they would sell it for a few thousand bucks. Well, Herman put it in his will that they would split the inventory, but only after I was allowed to have anything I could take in one trip. His attorney called me that afternoon to tell me about the will. He said I had to be there the next morning to take what I wanted. I had the keys to the store so I went in that night with a tape measure and a come-a-long winch. The store had everything else I needed. I measured; the store was thirty feet deep. I checked the front door and sidewalk before making my cart. I disassembled the inventory racks and used the framing to make the base of a cart twenty-nine feet, eleven and two-thirds inches long. It was forty-seven and seven-eighths inches wide. I attached ten sets of roller skates to the bottom. These steel skates allowed for the cart to be only one and a half inches off the ground. I used the steel shelving for the platform. On this, I could stack it seven feet, eleven inches high and still clear the door."

Peggy took a step back. "Wow, look at the time."

Rodger looked at the clock. "I spent the entire night loading the inventory onto the storage cart. Harvey, Stan, and the attorney opened the door the next morning. The entrance was completely filled by my fourteen-hundred cubic foot cart. I walked up and attached the come-a-long to the front of the cart. I had already attached it to a tree in the sidewalk. I began ratcheting it out and it would barely move because it was so heavy. I not only fit the entire inventory in it, but the computer, cash register, and the best shelving. Harvey said to me, 'What the fuck do you think you're doing?' Stan shoved me down on the sidewalk and kicked me in the face. The attorney yelled, 'Stop!' to Stan. With all the yelling, the cops quickly arrived. Stan was arrested for assault, cuffed and thrown into the back of the squad car.

"Harvey's face was red and the veins on his neck were bulging out. He pointed to me and yelled to the police, 'This asshole is stealing everything in my father's store. Why don't you arrest him?' The policeman held him back with a nightstick and said, 'Your own attorney says he has the right to take it.'

"I continued cranking the come-a-long handle for fifteen minutes until I got the cart completely clear of the store. I had arranged for a storage company to be there with a moving van and I put it in storage. I knew every collector who would be interested in the inventory. It took me the entire summer to sell it all, but when I was done I cleared two hundred thousand dollars."

Peggy said, "Really, two hundred thousand dollars? And what happened to Stan?"

"With his previous drug record, they gave him one year in county jail. Both of them left the area. I don't think they ever realized Herman wanted me to have it. It was just Herman's way of leaving one last challenge for me to remember him by, as well as playing a great prank on his asshole kids."

Rodger's phone rang.

"You better get that." Peggy quickly exited to the break room.

It was Steven Case, demanding Rodger come to his office now. Rodger put on his denim jacket and took two water bottles from his file cabinet and put them into his deep inside pockets. He entered Steven's office.

Steven said, "Sit down, Rodger," as he paced behind his desk and flipped the computer on. "What don't you understand about enough is enough? I have ordered you off the Stealth project, yet you insist on disrupting the project, me, and the entire staff about you own paranoid delusions."

Rodger interrupted, asking, "Can I get water?" Before Steven could respond, he walked to the bar refrigerator. He carefully examined the bottles caps before taking two and then slipped the two bottles out of his pocket and put them behind the other bottles.

Rodger had been sneaking deionized water from Space Key's clean room into Steven's refrigerator for months now. Most people have a misconception that water should be pure. They will buy bottled water to avoid any contamination or chemicals in their water. However, water is never pure in nature. Water is like a sponge, soaking up any minerals, chemicals, or contaminates it comes in contact with. It is a costly procedure to make water pure. Deionized water is so free of contaminates that its purity is measured in watts. Without any minerals, water will not conduct electricity. If you were in a tub of deionized water and an electrical cord fell into it, you would not get shocked. The minerals in the water are what conduct the electricity. The medical and electronics industries use it to clean their instruments and parts. The water sucks anything on the parts off. If you drank deionized water, it would suck vital minerals out of your body and eventually kill you.

"Shit, Rodger! Can't you sit still until I am finished?"

"OK. Do you want a water?" Rodger stepped behind the desk to set the water bottle down and catch the last couple of digits of Steven's password. Steven was still using his granddaughter's name for his password.

Rodger sat down with a satisfied smirk. He was convinced Steven had something to do with Xing Juan Zhang's murder. Xing Juan developed tracking software that Space Key sold to *Find It Now* for millions of dollars. It allowed *Find It Now* to direct ads to targeted groups based on the types of searches they had previously made.

The Chinese government had acquired the same software a week earlier, which enabled them to track the Internet usage of everyone in China. Rodger had been madly in love with Xing Juan, but she had no interest in an intimate relationship.

"This is your last warning," Steven said, while pointing his finger at Rodger. "If I see another e-mail from you, or you do anything to disrupt the project, I will fire you. Do you understand?"

Steven was breathing hard as he took a drink from the bottle Rodger handed him. Only a few months ago he was running marathons, but now he was weak. None of the tests conducted at the hospital could detect what was causing his deteriorating health.

Trying to be as serious as possible, Rodger said, "OK, I will stay out of the project." He paused. "Are you OK, Steven?"

"Yes, I'm OK. Now get out of here."

CHAPTER 13

A t quarter past noon, Irene knelt on the floor, opened the bottom drawer of an IBM copier, and loaded paper. The manager was in the back office and Jack, with the comb-over, was behind the counter, restocking the printer cartridge inventory. Irene pulled open the drawer of the next copier:

"How did my novel come out?"

Slightly startled, Irene turned around and stood up. Bill looked up to see her hazel eyes then looked down. Her bright yellow, six-inch platform shoes were scuffed from the floor. "Nice shoes," Bill said.

"Sometimes I like to see the world from up here." Surprisingly, she moved closer to Bill and noticed his aftershave. "Oh, my God, your book is so rad! I read it all night. Let me go get your order." She hurried around the counter, reached up for the copies, and ten plastic multi-colored bracelets slid down to her elbow. She placed the order on the counter and the bracelets slid back down to her hand. "OK, like when you first came in, I didn't know you could write... I mean the professor I work for has written books but, like... I don't wanta read them... It's all that government conspiracy shit. But like, wow, yours is so rad!"

Bill picked up a blue bound copy and opened it flat on the counter. "I like it! You did a great job. Can you get out of here for lunch?"

"Yeah, sure, I was hoping you'd ask again; anyway this place is dead today. Give me a minute to punch out."

Bill was excited, as his pickup lines never worked before. He just realized there were perks to being an author.

Bill held open the door of the Cattleman's Club for Irene and asked the hostess for a booth in the back. The restaurant was almost empty. He slid across the dark red leather upholstery until he was side by side with Irene. The high backs of the booth hid them from the four customers at the counter in the restaurant. "How do you like working at Kinko's?"

"It's OK. They're cool with working around my classes."

"What are you taking?" Bill asked.

"I'm a third-year lit major at San Jose State."

Bill ordered drinks. He thought, God, she is beautiful. I wish I could get her to kiss me. He finally put his hand on Irene's knee, and was surprised that she didn't push it away. He let it just sit there. "You obviously are doing something that you love."

"Well, yeah, I have put packages together for Professor Gorzynski." She stared into Bill's blue eyes. "How long have you been writing?"

Bill turned his hand over and ran the back of his fingernails lightly up Irene's leg. Irene straightened up her body and spread her knees apart.

Bill could feel his heart racing as he slid the back of his fingers higher up her leg, and just slightly brushed his fingers onto the edge of her panties. He responded while he left his fingers on Irene's thong, "This is the first thing I've written since college. I had been working as an engineer at Space Key until the dot-com bust. I was bored and decided to write this story."

Irene pulled his hand off her thigh. "You are so talented. I love the way you slowly build suspense. I can't wait to finish it. I read it until two in the morning until I fell asleep." She paused. "Oh, I made an extra copy so I could finish reading it. You don't mind? Do you?"

Bill placed his arm on her shoulder, pulled her close, and said, "I want you to read it. I'm honored. If you help me I will give you a credit as an editor on the book." He moved his hand back on her neck and pulled slightly.

Irene allowed herself to be pulled closer. "None of my professors who I've helped edit ever offered to give me a credit in the book."

Bill tilted his head and kissed Irene. He slid his hand under her blouse and slowly felt her nipple through her bra.

Irene placed her hand on Bill's lap and felt his erection and stroked it through his pants. He pulled his hand out from under her blouse and grabbed the table and started to pulse his hips.

Irene slid under the table, unbuckled Bill's belt, pulled down his zipper, pulled his dick out of the fly of his boxers, and slowly ran her hand around it.

Stunned, Bill tensed and caught his breath. No longer able to control himself, he grabbed a napkin to catch the outburst of seamen.

Bill put himself back together as Irene sat back up with a big smile on her face, "I always fantasized about doing that in a public place. It was a rush." She paused for a minute and asked, "Does Steven get caught?"

Bill straightened up and thought, what the hell is she talking about? The waiter returned with two beers. As he took a drink, he realized she was talking about the book. "Well-well, ah, ah, I don't want to spoil it for you. If I tell you, then you won't be objective and I want your honest criticism. You are a lit major and could help me a lot."

"But he's such a bastard. I don't know why Xing Juan loved him." The waitress approached. Irene ordered a spinach salad and Bill ordered a steak sandwich. "I just thought it was implausible that someone as smart and educated as her would risk her life for such an asshole."

Bill held his chin. "I never thought about that. You make a good point. I am so lucky to have met you. You probably know something about getting a book published?"

Irene moved closer to Bill and grabbed his head with both hands and French-kissed him.

"The professors I have, that's all they talk about. How impossible it is to get published. With agents, without agents; it doesn't matter. Professor Gorzynski even rolled up his manuscript and marked the envelope to the publisher 'Open immediately, FRESH FISH.' It didn't work. The publisher wrote back, *I would have preferred the fish.* It's really unfair. Monica Lewinsky gives the president a blowjob and gets a book deal out of it. Hey!" She chuckled. "His name is Bill too. Maybe if you do something so shocking to get into the news, you'll have publishers beating your door down.

"Where is the next Steinbeck or Hemingway gonna come from?" Bill thought for a minute. He grabbed Irene and gave her a robust kiss and said, "You're right!"

"What are you doing now?" Irene asked.

"Mostly working on this book," Bill said. "But I'm also tending bar on Murphy Avenue just to pay the bills."

"Any girlfriends?"

"No," Bill continued. "I'm in the middle of an ugly divorce. Unemployment is very hard on a marriage. How about you?"

"I've got a lot of good friends, but nobody serious." Irene paused. "Tell me more about the book. What are you going to name it?"

"Ah," Bill paused. "I'm not really good at that type of marketing stuff. What do you think?"

"Space Key! It's a no brainer!" Irene shouted out.

CHAPTER 14

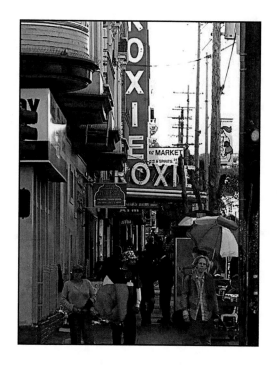

Summer 1978

At seven o'clock Monday morning Geary and Stockton Streets were busy with shoppers and people rushing to work. Thirteen-year-old Billy Giovanni stood in front of the City of Paris looking up and down the street. He put a dime in the *Chronicle* news stand machine and pulled out all twenty-five papers. Billy walked across the street to Union Square and yelled, "First Test Tube Baby Born. Get your *Chronicle*! Ten cents." In five minutes, Billy sold out his stack of papers. He had two dollars and fifty cents in his pocket when he jumped onto a bus to get to school. That afternoon in the Mission district, above the green awning of Joe's Market, hung a long-forgotten sign from a previous owner. Midnight-blue block letters over an orange background spelled out **REXALL DRUGS**. The three-story faded green Victorian had two flats above the market and a basement apartment below. Connected to the right was a similar building but with the Bulldog Baths, a gay bath house, on the ground floor. San Francisco had become a mecca for the gay community. This laid-back town was tolerant and gays from the conservative Midwest flocked here. To the left, *Annie Hall* lit up the marquee of the Roxie Theater. Every morning, the grocer rolled out two large wood-framed bins displaying a colorful array of fruits, vegetables, and cut flowers.

Colleen filled a brown bag with red grapes and picked up an *Examiner*. As she turned, a burly man with thick black hair covering his back and arms walked into the store wearing only a blond wig, calf-high white go-go boots and a pink G-string. He came out with a grocery bag and walked into the bath house. The red paint on the concrete floor was worn off in between the narrow aisles of groceries. The shelved wall behind the counter displayed wine, spirits, and cigarettes. Colleen placed the *Examiner* and grapes on the counter and said, "Hi, Ted, Who was that?

That's Bruce; he comes here almost every day this time. Nice guy. Buys wine and takes it next door.

"I guess that is why I love San Francisco. Never a dull moment. And can you give me a pack of Marlboros too, please."

Ted was Chinese, middle-aged, short, and had the most unusual eyebrows: just a half-inch long puff of thick, long black hair that darted out sideways above each eye like the plumb of a cockatoo.

"Oh, Colleen, you early today. You very pretty." He weighed the grapes on the scale, punched 75¢ into the register's ivory keys, and reached behind him and grabbed a pack of Marlboros. He pushed the $1.00 key, looked at Colleen, and said, "How your day?"

He looked at the *Examiner* and pressed the 10¢ key as Colleen said, "Shitty! I got fired today, for telling my asshole supervisor that he made an accounting error. I think he's stealing from the company. But thank you for asking."

"Very sorry," Ted paused. "One dolla ninety-six, please." Colleen twisted as she reached into the rear pocket of her bell-bottomed hip-hugger pants. Her bright red hair swirled forward.

Ted stared at the edge of her paisley halter top as it separated away from her side, exposing a few more freckles on her breast. "You find better job."

Colleen placed the correct change on the counter said, "Thank you."

Ted smiled.

Colleen walked to the side of the building, unlocked the gate, and walked down the stairs into the lower apartment. Inside it was bright, as only the front of the unit was below grade. The rear looked over the back of Potrero Hill, with a view of the Bay Bridge and Oakland. The oak hardwood floor was worn and the boards slightly cupped from years of San Francisco dampness. The narrow apartment was squeezed between two adjoining buildings. In order to bring light and fresh air to the kitchen and bathroom the building has a light well on each side. It is a four foot by four-foot tunnel that runs the entire height of the building opening at the top. On one side it's between the toilet room and sink and bath room. The Kitchen on the other side also had a light well but it only had one window. Colleen set the groceries on the hall table.

She opened the window which looked through the light well into the washroom and sat down on the toilet. The radio from the second floor was tuned to KSFO. Colleen listened to Gene Nelson introduce a new song by the Starland Vocal Band. Colleen was quickly humming along to the catchy jingle, *afternoon delight*. She wiped herself and flushed, walked down the hall into the washroom, and opened the window above the sink. She hummed along, thinking about grabbing her baby tight. The cool water turned her mood ring blue. She worried because Anthony would be angry that she was fired.

In the kitchen, she half-filled the chrome coffee percolator with water, added some Folgers grounds into the basket, and plugged in the pot. After opening the kitchen window, which looked into a light well next to the theater side of the building, she sat down to read the employment ads in the *Examiner*. She smelled the aroma of coffee as the percolator rattled with each eruption into the glass-knobbed lid. The radio upstairs went silent. She could hear footsteps and a door opening.

"Cool, man; you got Pong." Colleen heard from the light well.

"Yea, dude, you can turn it on while I roll the joint," a much deeper voice answered.

Colleen unplugged the noisy coffee pot, stood up, and leaned her head out the window.

"How do you turn it on?" It was her son Billy's voice.

"You need to put the TV on channel 3, and then it will work."

Colleen thought she had heard that voice before. She could hear the electronic pings from the game's paddles. A long pause was broken by, "I'm too fast for you." Now Colleen was sure it was the hippy who lived on the third floor. "Yah gonna like this shit. None of that leaf crap, all buds!"

Again, a pause, and she then heard him exhale and say, "Here."

Billy started coughing and the hippy said, "Pass the joint, bro." When Billy finally stopped coughing, the hippy continued, "Good shit, huh?"

"Yeah," Billy said, "Look at the pong ball, it's leaving a trail."

"Those are tracers, kid," the hippy said. "Hold your hand out like this and you can draw some in the air."

"That's cool. Pass me the joint."

This time Colleen couldn't hear Billy inhale and he only coughed once.

"How much for a lid?"

"Twenty bucks," the hippy said, "for a full three-finger lid."

"OK, but can you put a small amount of it into a separate bag for me?"

"No problemo but do you know how to roll a joint?"

Colleen could hear Billy, "No, could you do it for me."

"Sure, I'll roll you three joints and leave the rest in the bag."

"Cool, thanks man."

One hour later, Colleen heard her front door open and then the key drop on the hardwood floor. Billy's black hair hung down when he bent down. The huge bell bottoms of his jeans temporarily hid the key. He stood up and put the key into the pocket of his crumpled corduroy jacket. Six zits distorted his perfect pale face, which turned white when he saw Colleen.

"What's in your pockets?"

"Nothing. Why are you home?"

Colleen told him, "Let me see what's in your pockets."

"I don't know what you're talking about, Mom."

"You've been smoking pot!" Colleen said. "Your eyes are completely bloodshot."

"No, really Mom; it's just allergies."

"I can smell it." Colleen wrapped her arm around Billy's waist and patted each pocket until she felt the bag. Billy struggled with her, but Colleen pulled out the lid and said, "What? Do you think… I'm stupid?" She took it to the bathroom.

Billy screamed, "No mom, it's not mine," as Colleen lifted the toilet seat, unfolded the clear sandwich bag, dumped in the bag of marijuana and the three joints, and flushed the toilet. "I bought that for two kids in my class with their money. They're gonna kill me!"

"What the hell is going on?" Anthony said, as he swung open the front door.

"I'm handling it!" Colleen said.

Anthony marched down the hall and looked at the baggie in her hand. "Don't give me that shit!"

"If you must know, your little boy is dealing drugs." Colleen thought, Shit, why did I just say that to Anthony?

Anthony spun his head to look at Billy head on. "What's she talking about?"

Billy stood motionless until Tony grabbed his shoulders. "I bought some pot."

Anthony shook Billy. "She said dealing. She knows the difference."

Colleen stepped next to Billy and placed her hand between them. "I caught him with some pot, that's all."

"Don't you try to hide something. I know you're lying." Antony pushed Colleen's arm out of the way and said to Billy, "How long have you been smoking pot?"

"This is only the second time! Honest."

"Bullshit!" Anthony punched his fist into the door and squeezed Billy's face until tears flowed. "OK, where did you smoke it the first time?"

Billy cried, "Behind the backstop at the junior high."

"Who were you with?"

Billy turned his face away. "Just two other kids."

Anthony grabbed Billy's collar. "What two other kids? And don't lie to me."

"Julio and James, from the junior high."

"What were you doing with the pot today?" Anthony grabbed Billy by his hair and twisted it until his face was looking at him.

"They wanted to know if I knew where to buy some." Billy's scalp stung. "And I said sure. I was only helping out."

"You're lying! You're dealing drugs, and you're a liar." Anthony twisted Billy's hair tighter. Billy squirmed as tears rolled down his cheek. Anthony slammed Billy into the bathroom door, breaking the hinges. He continued to hold Billy's hair. "You are throwing your life away. Flunking school, smoking pot, dealing drugs. I'm going to put an end to this right now."

Colleen screamed, "You're hurting him! Stop this!" She was covered in sweat, face red and panting, as she hit Anthony's back with two clenched fists. "Let him go!"

Anthony pushed Billy away and looked at Colleen, "Or what?" He grabbed Colleen by her neck. "And what the hell are you doing home?" Colleen squeezed Anthony's wrist; her knuckles were white trying to lessen his grip.

"Answer me!"

"I got fired!" Colleen said as she struggled to push Anthony's hand away.

"You stupid shit; can't even keep a simple job."

"It wasn't my fault," Colleen said. "Harry's stealing."

"This entire country is corrupt." Anthony said. "You're no mother. You've got no discipline. Billy's flunked seventh grade. Now he's becoming a drug addict and a liar. See, I was right about Reverend Jones. We can only find peace through him." He dropped his arms and walked back down the hall and said, "I don't want you to talk bad about him again. I am going to see the Father. He'll know what to do. I'll be back. I'll ask him if we can live at the temple."

Peoples Temple mid 1970s 1859 Geary Blvd. San Francisco CA

When the front door closed, Colleen rushed to the bedroom. "Damn!" she said, as she pulled two suitcases and a surplus Army duffle bag from under the bed. "Billy, put your clothes and anything else you want in this suitcase."

Billy didn't move, but said, "What are you doing?"

Colleen screamed as she threw everything into the bags. "We can't be here when he gets back. Hurry!" She shivered and pulled the hood of a poncho over her head. Colleen feared Jim Jones. Anthony was a devoted follower, willing to allow Jones to control his life. Colleen knew the dark side of Jones and how he would beat members of the temple for not paying enough attention during his ranting sermons. Jones wielded power in San Francisco. He used his followers to act as an army of political volunteers. Mayor Moscone owed his election to Jones, winning by only 2,000 votes. Billy picked up a suitcase and took it to his bedroom and emptied his dresser drawer on the floor. "But I gotta go see James now!"

"Don't argue with me! We can't stay here," Colleen said, as she put their toothbrushes into the duffle bag. "Just hurry."

They both quickly threw clothes and personal items into the bags and ran from the apartment to the bus stop. The bus dropped them off at the Fourth and Townsend Cal Train Station. Old industrial buildings lined the north side of the tracks. The smokestack of the brewery was painted to look like a Hamm's beer can. Folger's coffee's neon sign displayed a giant tipping coffee cup. Sequential lights cascaded a neon drip of coffee down to a cup that spelled out, *GOOD TO THE LAST DROP*. South of the tracks, a bay inlet was the home of two ship repair docks. The gray warehouses' paint had peeled off and the weathered docks had missing planks. Colleen paid ninety cents for two tickets, and they climbed aboard the diesel-driven commuter train. A nonstop sprawl of industrial buildings lined the hour-and-a-half train ride down the San Francisco Peninsula until they reached Moffett Field. To the right of the railroad tracks, the fleet of P-3 Orion submarine chaser airplanes looked like toys against the background of the old dirigible hanger. To the left, dozens of workers climbed up and down three-legged ladders, filling buckets with dark red cherries.

"When I grew up down here," Colleen said as she squeezed Billy's hand, "the entire valley was orchards like that. We will be safe here, Billy." Colleen pushed at the duffle bag poking her leg. "I packed hangers. I can't believe it. Hangers." Billy started to smile, then turned his head away.

"Billy, why are you always doing something you know you shouldn't?"

"I don't know, Mom. It just gives me a feeling of excitement."

"You need to use better judgment. I think it is an adrenaline rush. You can also get that feeling by doing something constructive like playing sports."

"I hate playing sports. I suck at them. I am always the last one picked. When we played baseball at recess last week, most the girls were picked before me."

Coleen gave Billy a hug, "You will find something that you are good at."

Colleen and Billy got off at the Sunnyvale Station and walked one block to Murphy Avenue.

"Boy, it's hot here," Billy said.

"Yeah," she replied, "I forgot how nice the weather is in the valley."

Colleen was surprised to see only one block of the old Murphy Avenue still standing. Grisso's Mexican Market, Easy Loan Pawn Shop, a couple of restaurants, the Old Sunnyvale Theater, headlining *Behind The Green Door*, Kelly's Bar, and the Sunnyvale Hotel, with its sign, "Day, Weekly and Monthly Rates," still stood. The next five blocks up the street and three blocks to each side were freshly leveled dirt surrounded by a cyclone fence and a billboard with an artist's rendition of a new mall. Gone was the entire downtown: Woolworth's, Hart's department store, Kirkish's Western Supply, Foster Freeze, and all the beautiful elm trees that had graced the narrow grass park down the middle of both Murphy Street and Taffee Street.

"I can't believe it; it's all torn down. This was a beautiful downtown, Billy. They only left this old part of the street by the tracks."

Colleen and Billy stopped for a second to let their eyes adjust to the sudden dark inside the bar. Colleen spotted John, now an old man, tending the bar. His thick, white hair was combed straight back, and he was wearing a pink paisley, wide-collared shirt with the top two buttons open. He turned to look at the new arrivals. Colleen, duffle bag tucked under her left arm and holding a suitcase with her right hand, said, "Uncle John?"

"My God... Colleen! Is it really you?" John said, as he walked from behind the bar up to his niece. He threw his arms around her and said, "I'm so happy to see you!" He turned to face the bar and said, "Ignacio, Pat, Charlie, this is my goddaughter Colleen!"

"I didn't think it was possible for someone so pretty to be related to you, John," Charlie said as he lifted his beer.

Colleen pushed the back of her son's head. "This is Billy."

"Hi, Billy," John said. "Come in here so I can see you."

"Bill! My name is Bill," he said, as he walked forward, carrying the suitcase with both hands.

"Well, Bill, you are quite a good-looking young man." John put his arms around Billy to hug him, but Billy straightened up and leaned back, extending a hand. John shook his hand as he said, "I'm your Uncle John."

Colleen said, "Uncle John, I'm afraid I need your help."

John picked up her two bags. "Of course, darling, but there will be plenty of time for that. Let's put these bags in the back booth for now. You two look exhausted. Are you hungry?"

"I am." Billy looked at his mother.

"El Faro, the Mexican restaurant next door, has great food." John took a ten-dollar bill out of his pocket and handed it to Colleen. "And bring me back a chicken ranchero enchilada and a burrito for Ignacio."

Colleen was surprised to see Ignacio still working for John. She knew John had taken him in after his mother died. That was over forty years ago. His hair was still jet black, along with a thick mustache with a hint of gray roots, making it obvious he dyed his hair. Ignacio hugged Colleen so tight that she felt the metal buttons of his western shirt press against her ribs.

Two hours later, Billy sat with a stack of quarters at a table with a Pong game built into the top. John and Colleen sat across from each other in the back booth. Ignacio tended the bar with his half-eaten burrito on the counter next to his tequila on the rocks.

"How long has it been, Colleen?" John asked.

Colleen said, "Mom's funeral, ten years ago."

"I miss her," John said. "She had a hard life and is in a better place now."

"I never got to say goodbye," Colleen said. "I didn't even know she was sick. I just needed to get out of there, but she just couldn't accept that I had moved in with Anthony, an Italian no less. And then when we got into drugs¾" Colleen paused as tears filled her eyes.

"What's going on with you now?" John asked.

"Anthony and I got off drugs about four years ago." Colleen paused and shook her head. "But he became involved in the Peoples Temple. It's like he just traded one addiction for another."

John said, "I heard that Jim Jones is helping drug addicts stay clean. Even Rosalynn Carter has been on the news praising him for his work."

"I thought so, too," Colleen said, "when I first started going. Jones made me feel important and special. But he needs to control everything. Jones scares me. Something awful is going to happen. Anthony is brainwashed. He won't listen to me. All he talks about is when they are going to move to this tropical paradise in South America."

John tightened his grip on her hands as she cried.

"Billy has been getting into a lot of trouble. He flunked history and algebra and didn't get promoted. I caught him with pot today. I think he bought it just to get popular with some of his classmates but he has started smoking it too. Billy is shy and picked on at school. He gets beaten if he doesn't give the class bully his lunch money. Anyway, Anthony will use this to make Billy move to the Temple. I know three women whose children are at the Temple and they haven't seen them since. Jones sent them to Guyana to hide them. I know Tony is going to take Billy." Colleen started to cry.

John squeezed her hands. "I won't let that happen. You can stay with me a while but only until you get a job and find an apartment. Your father was an asshole to your mother. I was sorry to see that you were living with another asshole. I'll make sure Billy learns how to defend himself, too. Remember, I bought this bar by boxing."

"What happened to the downtown? I loved the stores and park in the middle of the street."

John shook his head. "The asshole real estate developers control the city council. They condemned the entire downtown except this end of Murphy to build a stupid mall. Most of my friends lost their businesses. I think they should all be shot." John became irritated just thinking about the way his neighbors' livelihoods had been taken away. He stood up and excused himself, explaining that he needed to make a few arrangements.

John pulled Ignacio's arm, leading him into the stock room. "Can you move into a motel for a month or two, until Colleen has a place? I'll pay for it."

"Of course, John; I just hope everything works out for Colleen."

John also pulled some strings with his friend, the school superintendent, to get Billy into the summer school program at Madrone Junior High. He lent Colleen his beloved 1975 Gremlin with its Levi's upholstery so she could job hunt.

★★★

Colleen spent the next three days responding to employment ads in the *San Jose Mercury News*. She set appointments to interview for accounting and office manager positions. She visited Libby's Cannery, Sunnyvale Jeep, Hewlett Packard, and a new startup company called Apple Computer. She filled out countless application forms but failed to get past the first interviews. Finally, on her way back to the bar, she saw a help-wanted sign in the window of Sunnyvale Business Machines one block north of the train station.

She walked into the cluttered store. The aroma reminded her of her school days when she would put freshly mimeographed handouts to her face and smell them. New Royal and IBM typewriters were displayed on the counter next to National cash registers. A sign on the wall read: We repair all brands of Typewriters, Cash Registers, Mimeographs and Dictaphones. Behind the counter, an elderly man wearing a blue shop apron unscrewed the bottom cover plate of a ten-key adding machine.

"Hello, I'm Colleen and I saw your hiring sign in the window."

Pete Gavin took off his reading glasses and asked, "Aren't you John's niece?"

She nodded her head as he continued.

"I remember when you were a little girl at Kelly's with your mother. You would play for hours with your Erector set."

"I forgot about that," Colleen said, "I loved that Erector set. Uncle John gave it to me for my seventh birthday but my father wouldn't let me play with it. He called Uncle John an asshole for giving me a boy's toy. He said it would turn me into a lesbian."

Pete smirked. "That sounds like your father."

"Yeah, Uncle John yanked it out of his hand and took it to the bar with him. I don't think they ever talked to each other again." She leaned her arm on the counter. "Mr. Gavin, isn't it?"

"Pete, call me Pete. Everyone else does. So are you moving back to Sunnyvale?"

"Only if I can find a job," Colleen replied.

"Well, I need someone, but finding the right person has been hard. You have to be mechanical to help with the repairs." Pete set down the screwdriver and pointed to the back. "But you also have to be good at keeping the books. Ever since my wife died three years ago, I have just been putting all the receipts into that file drawer."

Colleen looked at the half-opened drawer Pete had pointed to. The file folders stuffed with receipts and bills overflowed out the top, preventing the drawer from closing. She said, "I am so sorry about your wife. I didn't know."

"I miss her. She was a good wife and she kept everything organized for me. I never appreciated how much she did for me until..." Pete stopped and just looked at the open drawer.

Colleen finally said, "I have always been good at repairing stuff. I have my grandfather Daniel's blood in me."

Pete interrupted her. "I'm not worried about being able to teach you how to fix these machines.

After all, I saw all those machines you built with that Erector set of yours." Pete reached over and picked up an envelope. "This is from the IRS. I haven't filed my returns for the last two years and I don't know what I am going to do."

"Pete," Colleen said, "this is what I am good at. I started in accounting working for the *Berkeley Free Press* in 1971. Their books were a bigger mess than this and the government was looking for any excuse to shut them down. I recreated their books and the IRS wasn't able to do anything except hit them with a small fine for filing late. I will fix this for you. I also volunteered for George Moscone when he ran for mayor of San Francisco. I was the accountant for the campaign. I really like Mayor Moscone. But he constantly hit on me; he is such a womanizer. A married man yet he was often with seedy women."

"An angel must be looking down on me." Pete set down the envelope. "When can you start?"

CHAPTER 15

August 1978

John Kelly had a few too many Jamesons when he told Charlie that he had tickets for Sunday's 49er pre-season game with the Cincinnati Bengals. Charlie laughed as he said, "Your Niners are losers. The Bengals will blow them out."

"Bullshit. They're rebuilding; they have O.J. and Steve DeBerg is great. Do you want to put ten dollars on the game?"

Charlie polished off his drink. "I don't want your money. I will just give it back to you drinking. How about a real bet?"

"What do you mean?" John slurred.

Charlie motioned John to come closer. "The loser spends Monday in the bar in drag. How sure are you about your Niners?"

John, feeling invincible, said, "I would love to see you in a mini dress. You are on."

Little Pat Riley, the popular jockey, with a blue blazer and white fedora, sat at the bar listening to the bet. "I will make sure you have a full house on Monday"

That Monday, John poured coffee for him and Ignacio in the kitchen. "Shit, Ignacio, I made a bet that the Niners would win."

"So what?" Ignacio was very disinterested. "Do you want your eggs scrambled?"

"Yeah, thanks." John tied his shoe. "I need to go to Goodwill this morning."

Ignacio cracked six eggs while he sipped coffee. "I thought we got rid of all our old stuff last month."

"I need to buy a dress."

Ignacio set the bowl of eggs down and faced John. "OK, you got me. Why do you need a dress?"

"That was the bet. The loser comes to the bar today in drag."

Laughing, coffee came out of Ignacio's nose and he choked. "I'm coming with you. This will be fun."

"Bullshit! I don't know why I made the bet. How can I go into work in drag?"

Ignacio said, "You made the bet because you were drunk. You are not just going to put on a dress. I am going to fix you up. I can get some lipstick and mascara. You are going to be hot!"

John decided to make this a short day, coming in at 2:00 p.m. and hopefully leaving by five. Ignacio opened the bar himself for John at noon. Charlie and Pat were already there, waiting to see John.

"What, did John chicken out?"

Ignacio poured a drink. "John chicken out? In your dreams. He'll be in."

The bar was packed by two o'clock. Ignacio was having difficulty filling all the drinks. Bill had early dismissal and showed up at one to do his required studying. "Where's John?" he asked.

At 2:15, John snuck through the back door. He walked up behind the bar as if nothing were unusual. Everyone started laughing as John nonchalantly poured himself a Jameson. John wore a platinum blond wig, false dark eyelashes, deep red lipstick, and huge clip-on earrings. His evening gown had a gold halter top stuffed with red socks, which showed cleavage to his stomach. The white flowing silk dress just covered his knees. He wore fishnet nylons and gold sandals.

Little Pat Riley was able to stop laughing just long enough to say, "Marilyn, can you pour me one of those, too?"

Soon Mike and Charlie joined in. Pete said, "Hey, Marilyn, can you pour me a double?"

Charlie said, "Can I feel your doubles? I can show you a good time."

John put his hand under his false boobs. "You're not enough of a man for me," he quipped in a falsetto voice.

Everyone was having a good time. John hadn't had time to stop for lunch and gave Bill a twenty to pick up some food at El Faro's. A few minutes after Bill left on his errand, the front door was shoved open. Anthony Giovanni wore grease-stained blue Levi's, a soiled wife-beater shirt, and was unshaven. He walked up to the bar and said, "Who's Kelly?"

"Who's asking?" John said, as he filled a beer mug.

"I'm here to get Billy," Anthony responded, as he put his fist on the bar. John just waited, holding the mug until Anthony added, "Hey, I'm the fuckin' kid's father. I don't know what Colleen has told you, but I just want Billy. Where is he?"

"I'm John Kelly and you're not taking him!" John stood up straight in his Marilyn Monroe garb and set the mug down.

Anthony took a step back and lowered his hands. "I'm Billy's father and I am taking him."

John walked from behind the bar. "This is my bar and no asshole is taking him. Fifteen years ago, I should have never allowed a fucking piece-of-shit wop like you to take my sister's baby away."

Anthony made a fist with his right hand and started slapping it into his left palm. "I won't let Billy stay in a bar with you fuckin' homos."

Billy, with two bags from El Faro in his hands, stood in the entrance. John took another step toward Anthony until their faces were only an inch apart. "Listen, you fucking old fag," Anthony said, as he poked his finger against John's chest, "I'm here to take him back with me to the Temple where he will be around good people, not a bunch of drunks and perverts. And I'll enjoy beating the shit out of an old man."

John's adrenaline flowed. He could feel one more good fight in his blood. "You piece of shit, go ahead and try."

"No!" Billy screamed. He thought, I can't let Dad find me. He dropped the lunches and ran as fast as he could down Murphy Avenue.

Anthony saw his opportunity. One quick punch to John's face should take care of the old fag, leaving enough time to catch up to Billy and take him down to the Peoples Temple. He cocked his right arm and threw a punch at John's face. John turned sideways, absorbing the blow to his left check. His halter top ripped, and the red socks pushing out the breasts flew onto Pat's lap. Pat and Charlie jumped up to help, but before they were off their barstools, John countered with three lightning-fast jabs into Anthony's face. As Anthony tried to keep his balance, John punished him with a barrage of body blows directed at his kidneys. Anthony collapsed to the floor, curled up, holding his stomach.

John turned to Charlie. "Call the cops. Let's throw this asshole in jail."

Pat picked up the socks and handed them to John. "We can't have you topless. You might get arrested for indecent exposure." He regained his composure. "Let me get you some ice for your face."

"Thanks, Pat, but leave my face bloody until the police get here." John pushed the socks back into the top.

Within minutes, two patrol cars pulled up and four officers walked into Kelly's Bar. Officer Sean looked at Anthony laid out, groaning in pain, and then at John dressed as Marilyn Monroe with blood rolling down his cheek. "Let's get you a towel before you get blood on your dress."

Ignacio already had a bar towel ready with ice water.

Sean said, "You look great, John. What are you doing this Saturday night?"

John put the towel on his face. "I don't know. What did you have in mind?"

"What the fuck is going on here?" Anthony said. "Why aren't you arresting him? He beat the shit out of me."

Ignacio, Charlie, Pete, and Pat walked forward. Charlie said, "He hit him in the face; I saw it."

"Me too," Pat said.

Anthony was still laying on the floor in the fetal position, covered in blood. "He is keeping my son from me. You have to arrest him for kidnapping."

"You realize you picked the wrong old man to hit," Sean said. "You are making a serious accusation. What proof do you have?"

"Billy Giovanni is my son. Kelly is hiding him."

John put his hand on Sean's arm and said, "You've seen Billy here doing his homework. He and his mother Colleen escaped from this abusive asshole."

Sean gave Anthony a push with his foot, forcing him facedown, and cuffed him. "So, you're a real tough guy when it comes to pushing women and children around. I see you're not so good with an old man in a dress."

"Dammit. This drunk, perverted old man has been keeping my thirteen -year-old son in a bar." Anthony tried to roll over, but Sean kept him pinned with his foot.

John said, "Why don't you ask Anthony where he wants to take Billy?"

"I don't have to tell you anything!" Anthony said. "But, I belong to the Peoples Temple."

"I've heard of that," Officer Sean said. "Aren't you all moving to some place in the jungles of Guyana?"

"That's right," Anthony continued, "we can't live in this evil capitalist country where everything is about greed."

"I think six months in the slammer might do him some good," Sean said. "What do you think, John?"

Anthony interrupted, "I want an attorney now!"

"Well, if he wants to move to the jungle, why stop him?" John said. "Let's just make sure he goes alone."

Sean said, "Anthony, when do you leave?"

"Tomorrow night. I have a six o'clock flight."

Sean turned to John and whispered into his ear, "I'll hold him till then, and I will make sure he is on the plane, alone."

CHAPTER 16

olleen was at ease now with Anthony unable to contact her. She became indispensable to Pete's store, helping with customers and minor repairs, but she needed to stay late every night after closing. The IRS had been relentless, demanding fifteen thousand dollars, their estimate of unpaid taxes with penalties and interest. They threatened to seize the inventory. Colleen completed one year of Pete's taxes showing no tax liability, but she still had one year of receipts and invoices to reconcile with only one more month until the deadline. She and Billy lived at an apartment on Olive, one block from Murphy Avenue and two blocks from Madrone Junior High. Bill checked in with John every day after school. John made sure he had a lunch and made Bill study in the back booth for an hour every afternoon.

In 1976, Sunnyvale's city council acquired the entire downtown of Sunnyvale by eminent domain to make room for a new enclosed mall. There was much protest as it ruined businesses that had been there for thirty years. The project forced dozens of business to close, created dust, disrupted traffic, and interrupted business at the remaining shops. Only one block of old Murphy Avenue next to the train station remained. At midnight, the bar was empty, so John closed early. He walked up the dust-covered sidewalk of Murphy Avenue to the parking lot and stepped into the street to avoid the sawhorses which protected a freshly poured concrete section of sidewalk. The street lamp reflected brightly off the new, light gray cement, highlighting the words Bill Giovanni, written across the new concrete.

"That little asshole," John murmured as he shook his head.

★★★

Bill sat in summer algebra class staring at Maria and daydreaming. He had failed algebra and American history last year and needed to pass the summer classes. Maria's long, thick black hair cascaded down the right side of her neck as she studied her assignment. She was taking this class so she could take advanced classes in high school. Bill rehearsed in his mind how he would find a way to get her to like him. She saw him staring. Bill blushed, covered the zit on his chin with his hand, and looked down at his worksheet. Every time he tried to say something to her, his hands would sweat.

Today is the day I'll talk to her, Bill thought. After all, Maria had said hi to him a couple of times and once she'd even asked him, "How's it going?"

Bill could only answer, "Fine," then stood there too terrified to say another word. The bell had rung and Maria had grabbed her books and headed out.

Bill watched her go every day to Perfect Coffee at Fremont Corners. He caught up to her just as she was ordering a latté. "I'll have the same," he said across the counter to a Hispanic waitress. Bill bravely said, with a lump in his throat, "Oh. Hi, Maria; what's happening?"

"Not much since our class got out five minutes ago."

Bill was tongue-tied; she was so much smarter than him. When the counter girl handed them their coffees, Bill said, "Let me get this, Maria." He put a dollar and a half on the counter.

Maria said, "Thank you."

At the same time, the waitress said, "Gracias."

Bill wanted to say *de nada* but got confused with gracias and instead said, "Granada."

Maria laughed, "You just said pomegranate."

Bill's face turned red as he hurried out the door and he said, "I have to go help my Uncle John."

"Bill," John said as Bill opened the bar door, "how was school today?"

"Stupid, John. My teacher tried to get us to understand the math in solving the Rubik's Cube. I would like to tell him where to put that Rubik's Cube. By the way, a couple of my friends want to play some baseball and they really need one more player. Is it OK if I do my hour of studying when I get back?"

John put down his glass. "No! You can meet up with them in an hour."

"But all the other kids are meeting up now."

"Nevertheless, you have an hour of studying. When I see a good report card, we'll talk about it. And when I say a good report card, I mean As or Bs. Once you succeed, you will start to believe in yourself."

"May the force be with you," Billy said. "You must think you're Yoda or something," he added, as he walked to the back booth.

John said, "Do you know what happens when you don't study history?"

Bill looked confused. "No!"

"You repeat it."

"By the way, John," Bill said, "I called the Sunnyvale Police Department today to report that you have a minor in your bar."

"Oh, thank you," John said. "Who were you talking to? Because if it was Sean at dispatch, I need to tell him the poker game this week is at Chief O'Reilly's house."

★★★

The word Lucky, in green fluorescent lighting, lit up the top of the fifty-foot yellow-tiled tower in front of the Quonset hut-shaped supermarket. Behind the store, a long driveway lined by a cyclone fence led down to a loading dock. Wood cases stacked four high held the glass Coca-Cola bottles for return. Billy pushed a shopping cart down the ramp, grabbed the top case, and dumped the bottles into it. They clanked together. Billy quickly looked around. He wiped his forehead and emptied two more cases. His heart was pounding. This time, the sound of bottles was even louder. Billy looked around, grabbed the shopping cart handle, and pushed, leaving behind the last case. The cart was heavy but the adrenaline rush provided the strength to continue. Billy leaned his head down and pushed his arms forward, putting all his strength into pushing the shopping cart up the ramp. At the top, he quickly pushed the basket down the sidewalk of Evelyn Avenue for one block to Grisso's Market. He put the bottles into bags and loaded them into a Grisso's store cart. Inside, the checker racked the bottles into cases. Billy got paid 5¢ each for the one hundred forty-four bottles, a total of seven dollars and twenty cents. Sitting in the back booth, he smiled as he reached into his pocket and felt the crisp bills and the cool coins.Both the front and rear doors of the bar were held open with barstools. Inside, a box fan by the back door blew air into the room and an oscillating fan behind the bar blew air directly at Mike, making ripples through his curly black hair. He wore a blue pin-striped Dickie's work shirt. His orange hard hat was on the bar next to his Anchor Steam beer. "Damn," he said to Charlie, "it's hot out there. It's too damn hot to be working."

"Shit, Mike." Charlie took a sip from his martini. "You just stand around with a flag all day. You should try one of these, coldest drink in town. Besides that, it will grow hair on your chest."

Bill held a glass of Coke and looked up from the back booth, saying, "If he had any more hair, they would put him into the zoo."

John turned to Billy and said, "You're supposed to be studying."

"Bill," Mike looked toward his pants. "Do you got any hair down there yet?"

"Mike," John said, "I didn't know you were interested in little boys."

Bill laughed.

"Tell me, Bill," Charlie added, "do you have any girlfriends?"

"Not here, yet."

"Your mother told me that you have a poster of Marie Osmond in you room." Charlie took a sip from the martini. "Do you kiss her goodnight before you go to bed?"

"Don't worry about him stealing your poster, Bill," John said. "He kisses his poster of Donny when he goes to bed. Hey, Charlie, don't you even have a blow-up doll of him?"

Bill laughed. "Can I go play baseball now?"

Before John could answer, the phone rang. John picked up the phone just in time to hear the other end hang up. "Kelly's Bar," he said into the receiver as if someone were on the other end. After a long pause, he said, "I'm John Kelly, Officer; Bill Giovanni is my nephew." John paused again as the bar went silent.

Bill got up from the booth and stood next to the bar.

"Well, yes, Sergeant; I do watch him in the afternoon. He is here with me right now."

Charlie poked Billy with his elbow and whispered, "What are you in Dutch for this time?"

Bill looked at Charlie, raised his palms up, and shrugged his shoulders.

"I appreciate you calling, but I want to ask him first before I bring him down to the station." Again, John paused while he held the phone to his ear, looking directly at Bill. "Well, Officer, just because it is his name doesn't necessarily mean that he wrote it. I will ask him. If he did it, he will tell me the truth." John tightly covered the mouthpiece side of the receiver with the palm of his hand and said to Bill, "Did you write your name in fresh concrete last week?"

Bill stood speechless.

"Well, did you?"

"I did, Uncle John, but, but... I didn't think it was that big a deal."

John uncovered the mouthpiece and said into the phone, "Well, he admitted to it. I will bring him right down, Thank you, Sergeant."

As John hung up the phone, Bill said, "Uncle John, I'll pay for it. I'm sorry. I didn't think it was that bad."

"And how much money do you have?" John said.

Bill was shaking. "I got money."

"Mike," John said, "How much do you think it will cost to jackhammer up a sidewalk and repave it?"

Mike scratched his head. "Sounds like a full day's work plus a load of concrete. And don't forget the dump truck and dump fees. Maybe a thousand dollars, maybe more."

"Holy shit!" Billy said. "I don't have that much money."

Charlie said, "I don't think they will make him pay for it. They will probably just send him to juvenile hall until he's eighteen."

"Uncle John!" Bill shouted, "What am I going to do?"

"This is the first time you ever called me Uncle. Does it take a little fear of God before you show some respect?" A huge smile lit up John's face. "You're gonna learn that there's consequences to your actions. If you can't do the time, don't do the crime."

Billy's heart was pounding as he wiped his sweaty palms on his jeans. "What do you mean?"

Charlie laughed. "Don't you know when you've been hoodwinked?"

Billy looked up as John said, "There was nobody on the phone. I was just having a little fun with you."

"That's a good one, John," Charlie said. "Bill, you better check your pants before you go anywhere."

"Yeah, Uncle John, you got me pretty good. Can I go play ball now?"

★★★

As summer's end neared, Billy finished school with a B+ in both classes. Colleen finished Pete's taxes with Pete only paying nine hundred dollars in taxes and penalties. Now she was able to leave work at five p.m. when the shop closed. Bill continued to have lunch with Uncle John. Afterward, John taught Bill how to box.

"Don't stand facing me; you make a big target," John coached. "Stand sideways, left arm forward, and quickly jab at me."

John went into the back and pulled out his old speed bag and hung it in the back room. "You work ten minutes each day on the speed bag and your arms will get strong and fast."

Billy looked at the bag. "Ten minutes is nothing. Shouldn't I do it for at least a half hour?"

"OK, smart guy. I want to see if you can even keep hitting the bag for three minutes."

Billy struggled just to keep the bag moving and in two minutes, he said, "This is too hard. I can't keep the bag moving and my arms hurt."

"Move aside." John effortlessly had the speed bag flying between the rhythmic punches that he continued for ten minutes.

Billy was mesmerized watching his uncle make the speed bag almost dance. "That's incredible, Uncle John. I never seen anyone do that before."

"If you practice every day, you will get good at it and very quickly you won't have to worry about bullies."

★★★

Charlie was in his usual grouchy mood. "Can you believe it? Now we are wasting taxpayer money so Leo Ryan can go to Guyana because he suspects Jim Jones is holding the people against their will. Hell, they went with Jones and I don't want them back."

"Charlie," John said quietly, "don't say anything about this if Bill or Colleen are here. They would be terrified if Anthony came back."

"Uncle John," Bill shouted as he entered the bar, "What do you want for lunch today?"

"How about Tao Tao? I like their chicken salad. How about you, Bill?

"I think I'll get a beef burrito at El Faro," Bill replied, as he put his black sports bag and baseball bat down in the back booth.

John called in both orders and said, "Twenty minutes. It's always twenty minutes."

"Hey, Bill." Charlie wore a white shirt with powder blue cuffs and an unbuttoned, eight-inch wide, powder blue collar with a peace medallion on a thick gold chain. "Are you excited about starting school next week?"

"I hate school. It's stupid," Bill said.

"If you don't do well in school, then you will never get a good job," Charlie said. "What, you want to be a flag boy like Mike here?"

"Eat shit!" Mike said. "Working construction pays good and I have benefits."

"I worked construction for ten years," John said. "My father and I built this bar."

"You built this, Uncle John?"

"My father was the greatest craftsman ever. He rebuilt much of the Victorian woodwork in the San Francisco mansions and hotels after the earthquake," John said. "He was a grand man."

"Well, I am going to be a professional baseball player," Bill replied. "Reggie Jackson signed with the Yankees this year for almost two million dollars."

"OK, champ." John handed Bill three dollars. "Go get the food."

CHAPTER 17

Jackie Speier, twenty-eight-years old, a crimson blond with a huge, engaging smile, was the aide to Leo Ryan, the congressman from San Mateo, just south of San Francisco. She had just informed the congressman that Jim Jones might be practicing a mass suicide drill called the White Night. Although Jones was respected by most authorities and politicians, Congressman Ryan was concerned and decided to investigate.

"That settles it," Leo Ryan said. "I need to see for myself."

The next day, the *San Francisco Chronicle* headline reported: "Leo Ryan to go to Guyana." Colleen read the article, in which Ryan said that anyone wanting to come back could. Shit, what am I going to do if Anthony comes back? Colleen was paranoid that he would return and take away her new-found freedom. For two weeks, she would wake up in the middle of the night in cold sweats after dreams of him choking her.

On November 17, Congressman Leo Ryan, Jackie
Speier, and a few reporters landed at Port Kaituma's
airstrip in the jungles of Guyana. Ryan made it clear
that he would not be deterred from visiting the Peoples
Temple in Jonestown. The group rode in the back of
a dump truck seven miles more into the jungle to see
Jim Jones and his followers. Once there, every member
said that they were happy and wanted to stay. Jackie was
uneasy, as there was always either Jim Jones or one of
his leaders present. The next day, it rained hard, turning the entire camp into mud. Secretly, one member
after another told a reporter, Jackie, or the congressman
that they wanted out. Ryan called for a third plane to
meet them at the airstrip to accommodate those who
wanted to leave.

Once at the airstrip, Jackie heard screams and
gunshots. Armed men charged the planes and started
shooting. Terrified, Jackie dove facedown behind the
plane's wheel and acted as if she were dead. She continued to hear close gunfire. Suddenly, intense pain
overcame her as she felt five bullets rip into her body.
She continued to lie still as there was nothing else she
could do. After the assassins left, crawling, she looked
for Congressman Ryan and saw him also lying face
down. She hoped he also was playing dead, but as she
came closer she could see that he had been murdered.
A few of the surviving members of the Peoples Temple
pulled Jackie away from the plane and unknowingly
put her on top of an ant hill. Jackie was sure she was
going to die in this jungle. She lay there for an entire

day and night until the Guyana military arrived by plane. The only medicine they had were two aspirin. They flew her to Georgetown, where a U.S. military medevac plane was waiting.

On November 19, the Guyana military, highly armed, arrived at Jonestown to find over nine hundred bodies dead from a mass poisoning and most were children. News reached the world the next day.

Colleen and Billy were stunned with disbelief. Most of the victims were close friends. They were in shock for weeks. As much as they never wanted to see Anthony again, the loss of him and many of their friends haunted them. "Mom," Billy said, "I feel guilty because I wished Dad dead so many times."

"I know, honey. I wished him dead, too. You can't blame yourself, as he brought this on himself. Remember, he tried to take you with him."

Colleen hadn't been to church in years, but Saint Martin's Church was to have a remembrance for those lives lost at their eleven o'clock mass on Sunday. She and Billy attended, hoping to gain some closure to the loss they both felt. The service was moving and Colleen sang "Amazing Grace."

Monday, Colleen was back at work. On the radio, it was announced that Supervisor Dianne Feinstein of San Francisco would hold an unexpected news conference at twelve o'clock. City Hall was surrounded by police cars and rumors were flying.

At noon, Colleen watched channel 4 as Dianne Feinstein in tears stated, "As president of the board of supervisors, it's my duty to make this announcement: Both Mayor Moscone and Supervisor Harvey Milk have been shot and killed."

Colleen dropped into her chair in shock. George was a friend and someone she admired. San Francisco mourned for both George Moscone and Harvey Milk. Milk was the first openly gay elected official to hold public office in the United States. He became a martyr for the gay rights movement and an icon in San Francisco. Dan White, a disgruntled ex-supervisor with the city, opposed gay rights and resigned his position in protest to Mayor Moscone and Harvey Milk's liberal policies. He served one year, being found guilty only of involuntary manslaughter after his team of lawyers created what was often labeled the Twinkie defense. Shortly after his release, he committed suicide.

CHAPTER 18

August 24, 2000

"You owe me, Charlie," Bill shouted as he entered the bar.

A cool evening breeze chilled Kelly's Bar when Bill opened the door. Charlie looked up. "You were right about Woody. He had the Dodgers swinging off balance all night. Gary Sheffield told the reporters that Woody is a nothing pitcher. When asked why he was oh for five, he said, 'Fuck You, everyone has a bad night.'"

"I can't wait till Lawrence comes in."

Bill got behind the bar. "How's your drink, Charlie?"

"Empty, you stupid shit!" Charlie answered. "And Sheffield was swinging like a girl."

"What's wrong with how girls swing a bat? Shit, I bet I can hit a ball farther than any guy here." Florence set down a *National Enquirer* on the bar and stood up, showing off her lean, yet voluptuous body.

"Girls play softball," Charlie said. "Shit, Little Steve Wonder could even hit one of those."

"You stupid old man; why do I even talk to you?"

"I always figured that you've been coming in here all these years hoping I would ask you out."

Florence took a sip of her drink. "If it wasn't that Bill makes the coldest martini ever, I would be outta here."

"You should have had one when his uncle had the place."

Bill began mixing both Charlie and Florence another drink. It was early and Charlie, Pat, Tony, and Florence were the only customers in the bar.

"Hey, Charlie," Florence said as she picked up the *Enquirer*, "there's a liquid diet in here. I figure you should have lost a pound a week for... how many years have you been coming in here?"

"Thirty!" Charlie said, as he placed both hands on his potbelly, "and proud of it."

Lawrence entered the bar with the *Sunnyvale News* open to the headline: "Man dies in Kelly's Bar." "Bill, have you poisoned anyone... lately?"

"Hey, that's not funny," Bill answered back. "I'm still upset about what happened. I didn't know him well, but Paul was a customer."

Charlie said, "Well, it's too late to worry about it now. He was a fuckin' freak and now he's a dead fuckin' freak. Why don't you call the coroner's office?"

"Nah, I don't want to get involved," Bill answered.

"What! You just said you're upset. You feel bad that you never really knew him. What an asshole you are. The cops gave you the number. You can see if he had money. Tell them you want to file a claim against his estate. He still owes you for your fuckin' tip."

"I want to know what you told Ignacio," Lawrence said. "'I killed one of your customers.'"

"I'm glad you think this is so funny. Geez, the guy had been coming in here for years and we didn't know anything about him."

"Well, shit! You sanctimonious asshole! I've been coming in here since your Uncle John owned the place and you did your homework in the back booth." Charlie took a drink. "And what the hell do you know about me? What do I do for a fuckin' living?"

"Gee, well, I always just figured that you were some sort of executive or supervisor where you didn't have to work very late anymore," Bill responded in a defensive manner.

"Yah see, you don't know jack about anyone who comes in here. I don't come in here to get interrogated. I could go home for that. I come in here to get a buzz and to bullshit with someone who won't nag me."

"What type of job do you have?" Bill fidgeted with a bar towel, folding it into a neat triangle. "I mean if you want to tell me."

"I've had the same bullshit sales position with the same fuckin' insurance company for twenty-five years. I sell insurance, annuities, and any fuckin' investment program that pays commissions. The job sucks! I hate it. I do paperwork in the office every morning but then have to wait until the evenings to meet with my clients at their homes after they come from work. I was going to retire this year but the dot com bust killed my mutual funds, They aren't worth shit right now. Are you going to call the coroner or not?"

Tony said, "Charlie, if you want something more in life, you should come to our church with me this Sunday."

"What! You believe in that shit?" Charlie yelled back.

Tony set his beer down and put his hand on Charlie's back. "Yes, I believe. Every time I have prayed for something, God has answered me."

"I believe too, but I learned you must be careful what you pray for." Charlie paused as he took a drink. "When I was just a stupid teenager, I prayed to God every night for a BIG DICK. He answered me all right... in 1968, Nixon was elected president!"

Tony swiped his arm across the bar, and as his and Charlie's drinks flew across the room, he stormed out, saying, "You're all going to hell!"

Charlie turned to Lawrence. "I don't think Tony thought that was funny. Some guys just don't have any sense of humor."

"Hey, Lawrence," Bill whispered, "have you ever been in an awkward situation and needed some professional help?"

"Say, shit, are you in trouble or are you trying to keep out of trouble?" Lawrence said.

Bill stood motionless for half a minute. "A little of both."

"Well, my mouthpiece is Joe Black," Lawrence said. "He doesn't care what I do for a living. Actually, he gives me advice on how to be a bookie without getting busted. The last time I was arrested, he got the DA to drop the case if I agreed not to sue the police department. He made me look like Mother Teresa." Lawrence pulled Joe Black's business card from his wallet and handed it to Bill.

"Hey," Bill said to Florence, "let me see that *National Enquirer*."

CHAPTER 19

Friday night at the Music Tunnel, Bart had the kara-oke machine blasting the music to "Mamas Don't Let Your Babies Grow Up to Be Cowboys," as two Asian men sang out of tune. The bar had a long counter kitty-cornered at the front. The room widened to a dance floor, which would only fit four dancers, and two pool tables in the back. Twelve men and two girls with them crowded the bar. Henry sat on the barstool next to Rodger. He wore blue jeans, black Adidas shoes with white socks, and a black Prince of Persia sweatshirt with food stains on the picture. His black, gelled hair was combed back. "I just downloaded the game *Leisure Suit Larry, Magna Cum Laude* last night and played it until four in the morning. Man, I am so burnt today."

Rodger continued to swirl his glass of dark beer when Henry added, "Man, the graphics are unreal." When Rodger didn't respond, he said, "What's up with you?"

Rodger finished the beer in one gulp. "I just found out this morning that my best friend from college, Paul Miguel, died last week. He choked to death on a peanut in a Sunnyvale bar."

"That's horrible," said Jenny, a tall, bleached blond part-time bartender. Her tight, low-cut blouse barely covered her breasts. "I'm sorry about your friend. How long ago were you in college?"

"Paul Miguel and I went to Berkeley in the late sixties." Rodger drank the rest of his beer and thought, first Xing Juan and now Paul. I don't have anyone left.

"Do you guys want another round?" Jenny asked.

Rodger just stared at his empty beer glass.

She continued, "You went to Berkeley? Were you a hippy?"

Rodger nodded. "I had long hair, like everyone else, and I went to a lot of the protests. I even got arrested at a sit-in. But I wasn't a fanatic. My best friend Paul was. He wanted to bring the government down. He was still that way. He was always telling me that I was a sellout and should quit working for Space Key. He called them a war monger. Ya know that I only have four more years and I can retire, but I don't know if I can make it that long. I think Paul was right. When I started with Space Key, the company was still small enough to be exciting to work for. Every Friday at noon, Dave Key, the company CEO, would bring in kegs of beer and he would barbecue steak sandwiches for everyone. He was just as shit-faced as we were by four-thirty. I worked nonstop producing their first missile guidance software. I was The Man. When they merged with WAD, I should have quit."

"That's just the way it is," Henry replied. "Every company is bullshit. I don't give a shit about my job."

"I hadn't heard from Paul for a week, which was unlike him. I went to his apartment and it had a yellow tag on it, stating 'Do not enter by order of the San Jose police.'" I went to the station only to find out he was in the morgue. His family wouldn't come out from Wisconsin to identify the body so I had to do it. I have never been so creeped out in my life. They gave me his keys and had an officer accompany me to the apartment. When he didn't find anything of interest, he left me there by myself. I took a couple of paintings he made. They aren't very good and he didn't paint for very long before getting bored with it.

"I looked over his desk and there was a notebook half-filled with the last couple of conversations I'd had with him about Space Key. I opened his bottom desk drawer and found forty more notebooks detailing every conversation I'd had with him about Space Key. There are twenty years of my conversations in those notebooks. We drank a lot and I had told him things I shouldn't have. A lot of this is classified information. He had remembered the source code calculations I designed for the ultrasonic testing. He hated that because he thought we were killing whales. He also wrote about Xing Juan Chang being murdered in Hong Kong. He wrote that she was selling classified information to the Chinese and someone murdered her for what she was carrying. I have no idea what he was planning to do with this, but I am glad I got to it before anyone else."

"Do you guys want another round?" Jenny asked.

Henry said, "I would like a round with you."

Jenny stood up straight. "In your dreams, Henry; besides, you couldn't handle me."

Rodger laughed. "When I was at Berkeley, it was Free Love; nowadays, Henry has to pay fifty bucks for software to see Leisure Suit Larry get fucked."

Henry's face blushed red.

Jenny moved forward, bending over the bar so that her cleavage was directly in front of Henry's face. "These are the real thing."

Henry turned even redder as Rodger laughed harder and said, "Jenny, you are the hottest. I'll have another Anchor... and give Henry a Bud to cool him off."

★★★

That evening, Johnny was in bed and Mary sat on the sofa chewing a torn cuticle while reading from the laptop. Bill came in with a stack of blue bound copies of the book and a *National Enquirer* and put them on the couch next to Mary. "They came out good," he said.

Mary picked up a copy and quickly flipped through the pages. "Yeah, it came out nice, but what are you going to do with them?"

"I told you that I will sell our book," Bill said, "and I will. I named it *Space Key*."

"There's dinner on the table," Mary said, as she tapped her finger on the laptop. "I don't want to burst your bubble, but getting a publisher to read a manuscript is almost impossible."

Bill sat down at the kitchen table. "Will you please take that optimistic attitude of yours somewhere else?" Bill cut the baked potato on his plate, covered it with butter, and took a bite from a deep-fried chicken leg and said, "I'm divorcing you, Mary."

Mary put down the computer and walked into the kitchen. "What are you talking about?"

"Can't you see I'm eating here?" Bill said, with a mouth full of chicken. "Good chicken."

Mary poured herself an iced tea and said, "Do you want a beer?"

Bill wiped his mouth. "Yeah, thanks."

Mary gave Bill an Anchor beer from the frig, sat down next to Bill, and tapped her finger on the table. "What are you talking about?"

"I'm divorcing you, Mary." Bill paused and watched Mary take a sip of her iced tea. "You are right about the story he wrote, in that I could never just get it published. It's the best way to make this work."

Mary set the glass down. "To make what work?"

Bill took a drink of beer. "To sell our book."

"Wa… wa… what the hell are you talking about?" Mary stuttered and she got up and paced around the table. "I think you finally have lost it. I should just throw your ass out of here."

"That would be a good start, really!" Bill said.

"This isn't funny anymore. Just shu… shu… shut up!" Mary stammered.

"You gave me the idea," Bill responded. "You said nobody will buy a book from a new author unless it's someone in the news. Well, our divorce will make national news. You can go on *Oprah* or something. It would be great headlines: *DUMPED WIFE SUES FOR HUBBIE'S BOOK!*

"It's not that easy," Mary said. "You can't just sell someone's book like it's yours."

"Yes, I can," Bill said. "I called the coroner's office today. They checked for relatives of Paul Miguel and all they could find were his father and sister in Wisconsin, who hadn't heard from him since he dropped out of Berkeley thirty years ago. The guy was a hermit. This is our big break."

"I don't know," Mary said.

"All you have to do is go on some talk shows and make me out to be a real asshole."

"I don't have to pretend that you're an a-a-a-asshole," Mary responded, "but I don't want to divorce you."

"We don't have to go all the way through with the divorce. You just need to get some media attention. After all, you work at Space Key. You claim the story came from you and I just did the typing." Bill stood up and put his arms around Mary as she circled the table. "You just need to keep up the act long enough for me to sell the book. It could be worth thousands if we get enough publicity. Then we can reconcile on *Dr. Phil.*"

"You think this is funny, don't you?" Mary said. "It will never work. Besides, Johnny is having problems and now you want to do something like this."

Bill tried to kiss Mary on the lips but she turned her face, so he kissed her cheek. "Lawrence gave me the name of his attorney. This guy can fix anything. I see him tomorrow."

Mary slammed her glass on the table. "You ASS HOLE. You did this without even discussing it with me. And you expect me to be lovey dovey? Get the hell out of here."

"Good, that's the spirit," Bill said. "You really sound pissed off."

Mary walked out of the kitchen with her eyes watered up and said, "G-g-g-g-get the hell out of here now!"

Bill grabbed a jacket and said, "I'll call you tomorrow," before he closed the door behind him.

CHAPTER 20

October 2, 1985

It was eight a.m. October 2, 1985, Bill's twenty-first birthday. Bill was at Kelly's cleaning up and icing up the martini glasses. George of South County Beverage Supply walked in with his clipboard in hand and scanned the shelves. "It looks like you had a good week."

"I think so," Bill said. "I know Ignacio has been exhausted lately. I think he's getting too old to keep up this pace."

George went about his business removing the empty kegs and restocking the bar. He kept track of the inventory on a carbon paper form clipped to a metal clipboard. He used a calculator to total the invoice and handed it to Bill to sign.

"You tell Ignacio that George says it is time for him to take it easy. I think you can run the bar."

"OK, George, I will and thank you."

Ignacio arrived at ten a.m. with a birthday cake and a present for Bill. "Happy birthday, Bill. This is a big day for you."

"Thank you, Ignacio, but I don't feel any different."

"You're twenty-one now, Bill. How would you like to try your hand at bartending?"

Bill hesitated. "I don't think so, Ignacio." He gazed toward the floor. "I can't talk to strangers."

Ignacio slapped Bill on the back. "Don't worry about that. When your Uncle John first got me to bartend, I was terrified. Once I got going, it became fun. Your Uncle John can't work anymore and I'm getting too old to stay up all night. I need your help. Come in at nine and you can close."

"Well you aren't the only one who thinks so. George told me that I should be running the place," Bill reluctantly agreed as he opened his present. "Wow, Ignacio, a Nintendo! You shouldn't have, but thank you."

Bill showed up at the bar at eight-thirty worried about having to wait on the customers.

Ignacio said, "Don't worry, Bill. This is your home and you will be fine. If the customers are making noise and arguing, you are doing a good job. That is why they come in."

Bill washed some glasses and got another bag of peanuts from the back room.

Channel 7 news was on the TV above the bar with the volume turned down. The text crawler across the bottom announced "Rock Hudson dies of AIDS."

Ignacio handed Bill the Old Fashioned he made and told him to give it to Charlie. He then turned up the volume to hear the story. Peter Jennings, the network anchor, said that Rock Hudson, leading actor from the 1960s and '70s who starred in thirty-five films, had died at Saint Luke's Hospital from complications due to AIDS. Reaction from Hollywood showed concern from actresses who had costarred with him. Morgan Fairchild was quoted as saying, "Rock Hudson's death gave AIDS a face."

Bill set the glasses down on the bar, "Ignacio, how many of yours and Uncle John's friends have died?"

"At least half of our gay friends. It's horrible, especially in San Francisco. So many of them came to the City because of how accepting the people were. You can't be gay in Kansas. But now nobody wants to be near us. A bunch of teenagers threw rocks at me the last time I went to visit a friend in San Francisco.

Bill gave Ignacio a hug. "Everyone has become paranoid. Poor Ryan White who is only thirteen got Aids from a transfusion. Indiana won't let him attend school now. The doctors said there is no risk but everyone is scared."

Charlie yelled across the bar at Bill, "This is the first time that the customers need to check the ID of the bartender."

Bill shouted back, "You senile old fart. I want to see the pass that let you out of your nursing home."

"I'm going to report Ignacio to the child labor board," Charlie responded.

"You're just jealous, Charlie; the last time you had some young pussy, FDR was president."

As Charlie laughed, he said, "Is your girlfriend twelve yet?"

Bill realized he was having fun trading spars with Charlie. He had never felt comfortable conversing with adults, but this was different. It was a game. "Can you still get an erection at your age, Charlie?"

"Well, sometimes I need the help of a popsicle stick and some duct tape but I've never had any complaints." Charlie finished off his Old Fashioned. "After you put your tricycle away, make me another. And don't make it like Ignacio; put some booze in it."

Ignacio looked at Bill. "I think you have this under control. I'm going home to check on John."

Around ten that night, Angela showed up wearing a paisley halter top and skin-tight jeans. She sat at the bar and ordered a martini. Bill set the drink on the bar, observing her large breasts bursting out of the side of her top.

"Where's Jake?" Bill asked. Jake and Angela were regulars on Friday nights after their dinner.

"That piece of shit." Angela downed the martini in two swallows and set the glass down with the ice still stuck to the inside of the glass. "Give me another."

Bill poured her another in a new glass. Angela said in a loud, angry voice, "That asshole told me he had the flu so I decided to go see *Out of Africa*. As soon as I walked into the theater, I saw him in the back row making out with my best friend, Toni." She drank what was left in one swallow. "That slut!"

Bill picked up her empty martini glass. "Well, at least you found out. You're better off without him."

"Fuck you! Just give me another"

Charlie said, "Even on your birthday, women don't even want to talk to you."

Angela grumbled, "I didn't mean to be such a bitch to you, especially since it's your birthday. How old are you?"

"Twenty-one. That's why Ignacio let me tend bar tonight."

Bill worked until two a.m. before he closed the bar. He couldn't believe the adrenaline rush he was having making jabs with the customers and them vying for his attention. And he had two hundred dollars in tips in his pocket. Angela was still at the bar and in a talkative mood after four hours of martinis. "Come on, Bill; I don't want to leave. You are the only friend I have."

Bill locked the door, turned off the outside lights, and sat next to Angela. "What am I going to do with you? You're too drunk to drive home. I can call you a cab or I can drive you home myself."

"Why don't I be your birthday present?" she slurred. She put her arms around Bill and kissed him. Bill was turned on. He was shy with women and still a virgin. He had never had someone seduce him. He let her kiss him and was surprised when Angela reached down and felt the boner in his pants. She stood up, grabbed Bill's arm and led him to the back booth. Bill told her, "Just a minute," and went into the bathroom to get a condom from the machine. He turned on the radio to Madonna singing, Like a virgin, thinking he had been touched for the first time. How ironic.

Angela pulled Bill's pants down. Angela stroked Bill's dick and started to lick it. Bill was embarrassed because he didn't know what to do. Should he take off Angela's jeans? Fortunately, Angela had no problems in knowing the procedure. She pulled her own jeans down. She grabbed Bill's hand and placed it in her vagina and guided his fingers to her G-spot and showed him how to stroke it. Angela took the condom from Bill, ripped the package open, and unrolled in onto Bill's penis. Bill came in the condom before she had completed putting it on. Bill was embarrassed and he wasn't sure what to say or do.

"Do you want a ride home?"

Angela said, "Sure, you're no fun anyway."

The next morning, Bill woke up with a small hangover and was still tired from his long night. He put on some clothes and walked into the kitchen. His mother Colleen sat at their yellow Formica kitchen table with her Texas Instruments 1100 calculator and a stack of receipts and invoices in front of her.

"Mom," Bill said, "you have to stop working so hard."

Colleen looked up. She was already dressed in a white blouse and black skirt. She was still an attractive woman, her naturally curly hair now still red due to hair dye. The only hint of her being in her mid-fifties was the wrinkles around her eyes. "Happy birthday, Bill. I didn't get a chance to tell you yesterday with you working. I have a present for you." She handed Bill a large box wrapped in red and yellow paper. Bill opened it to find a black leather sports jacket.

"Thank you, Mom. How did you know that I wanted a leather jacket?" Bill put the jacket on and it fit perfectly. Finally, he couldn't contain himself. He excitedly told Colleen how great he had felt bartending. "I felt important and everyone in the bar wanted my attention. I've always been shy, but last night I was the life of the party."

"You've always been important," Colleen said, as she poured her coffee. "Maybe you just found yourself."

CHAPTER 21

August 29, 2000

The law office of Joe Black was on the seventh floor of the De Anza building across the street from Saint James Park in San Jose. Bad Boy Bail Bonds and Zig Zag Bail Bonds occupied the two dilapidated buildings on the right side and Santa Clara County's jailhouse was to the left.

Bill entered the office and the receptionist, Vicky, stuttered, "Can I help you?"

Bill stared at her low-cut white lace blouse that barely concealed her nipples. She let Bill into the back office, her black high heels tapping on the floor. Joe Black sat in a red leather swivel chair behind a walnut desk inlaid with gold on the sides. Law books filled the dark wood bookshelves behind him. He stood up when Bill entered the room and extended his hand across the table as Bill said, "Mr. Black, Lawrence recommended me to you."

"Call me Joe." He wore a hand-tailored leather sports jacket, a Kelly green dress shirt with black pin-striped suspenders, and a matching Kelly green triangle-folded handkerchief protruded out of the jacket breast pocket.

Bill switched the blue bound manuscript he was carrying to his left hand and shook Joe's outstretched hand, saying, "Thank you," and he sat down.

"What can I do for you?" Joe asked, revealing his New York accent.

"I need an attorney to handle my divorce," Bill said.

"Didn't Lawrence tell you what type of law I practice? I don't handle divorces," Joe said, as he stood up to show Bill out.

"Let me explain," Bill said, as Joe sat back down. "I wrote a book and I only want to pretend to divorce my wife to get publicity to sell the book."

Joe set his elbow on the desk and rolled his hand as he said, "Get to the point."

"I want my wife to sue me for the rights to the book," Bill continued. "I figure it would make a good headline. You know: "Wife sues hubby for book rights.""

Joe scratched his head. "The only time I was in divorce court was for my own divorce ten years ago. Is that your book?" Joe asked.

"Yeah. It's a spy mystery that takes place at Space Key. I think it is pretty good." Bill handed him the copy. "Lawrence tells me you're the best. You can make anything happen."

Joe flipped through the pages and said, "I would need a six thousand-dollar retainer. What made you use Space Key as the setting?

"That's where my wife works," Bill said. "She is always telling me about what goes on there."

"That's good. I can use that. I might agree to represent your wife. But let me read some of this tonight before I agree to this. I want to see if it's any good."

Bill stood up to shake hands and said, "I'll be staying at the Hacienda Motel."

The Hacienda was on Taaffe Street, within walking distance to Bill's house and Kelly's Bar. With only one car, he needed to be close enough for when Mary needed it. The motel had been built in the early fifties, with a small pool in front surrounded by cracked concrete and a cyclone fence. The center driveway separated the two rows of bungalows with a parking place in front of each one.

Bill entered the small office. Aniel Patel entered from the owner's apartment connected to the rear of the office. Bill asked what discount he would get for a weekly rate and paid for the first week. He opened a bottle of Gallo Burgundy and started to read *Space Key*. After Irene had asked him, "Why did Xing Juan love Steven?" he knew he needed to read and learn the novel. He quickly discovered why Mary and Irene loved the story. It described the culture at Space Key and the plot kept him wanting to read more. He read over a hundred pages before the wine took its effect.

CHAPTER 22

Wednesday

The wind blew the front door open when Bill turned the key. "Johnny, are you ready for school?"

"Where were you, Dad?"

"Working! Get your shoes on." Bill walked back to the bathroom.

Mary was having her morning battle of the hair. "What are you doing here?"

"Oh, come on. I told you that we're not really getting a divorce. I will be here for you." Bill placed his hands on Mary's hips and kissed the back of her neck. Mary tilted her head forward. Bill kissed higher up her neck and moved his hands up her waist and under her blouse. Mary stopped his hands with hers and said, "Where did you spend the night?"

"I'm renting a room by the week at the Hacienda Motel." Bill pushed his hands farther up her blouse. "I only have to make it look like we're divorcing."

"Well, isn't that nice," Mary said, pulling away, "but I'm already going to be late for work. I know what you're trying to do. It's just that I'm afraid we w-w… w… we're gonna get caught."

"I talked to Joe Black yesterday. He's going to set the whole thing up if he thinks the book is any good." Bill stepped out of the bathroom. "I'll take you to work and Billy to school."

Mary rapidly tapped the brush on her palm. "How long do we need to keep this up?"

Bill smiled and grabbed her two jerking hands, holding them together. "A month… maybe two. Tops!"

After Bill dropped Mary off at work, Johnny was staring out the El Camino's window and asked, "Dad, what makes wind?"

"Trees do. This time of year, all those leaves on the tree make the branches heavy. The weight makes them wave like giant fans. You see those trees over there just swinging their branches? After a while, when enough of the leaves blow off, the wind will stop."

Johnny continued to look out the window at the gusting wind when Bill asked him, "How's school?"

Johnny shrugged his shoulders. "OK, I guess. I'm going to Mike's tonight for a sleepover. He's got Nintendo and a swimming pool."

"That sounds like fun." Bill rubbed Johnny's head. "Noogie patrol! Noogie patrol!"

★★★

Bill tossed a packed suitcase onto the El Camino's seat and then walked to Starbuck's via McKinley Street. Friday was garbage day on McKinley. He found a $274 cash receipt for a chainsaw from Orchard Supply and Hardware and put it in his pocket. At Starbuck's, he ordered two cups of caramel cappuccino and walked to Kinko's. "I got you a cappuccino," he said to Irene.

Irene turned around. She had accented her skin-tight capris with a six-inch-wide black vinyl belt below her hips and a black tube top. "You're so sweet. Thank you."

"Milton Mapes is playing at the Make Out Room on Friday night. Wanna come?"

"Who is he?" Irene asked.

Bill held his hands outstretched. "They're an awesome rock band out of Austin. Last year, I walked into the club late and only caught their last couple of songs. This year, I want to be there for the whole set."

"I would love to, but I'm not twenty-one yet."

"Don't worry about it. I'll pick you up tomorrow at eight."

Bill went shopping before going back to the motel. He emptied the suitcase and put two six-packs of beer and a bottle of margarita mix in the small refrigerator. He opened the box of condoms and emptied them into the nightstand along with a BIC[a] lighter, a box of chocolate truffles, and a stack of CDs. He put his boom box on the dresser along with incense. He rolled four joints and hid them inside a pair of rolled socks. Bill felt like a little kid having to wait a day before going to Disneyland. He was excited about playing the role of an author and having Irene, a young, hot girl, interested in him. He spent the rest of the afternoon reading *Space Key*.

Later, Bill walked into the house, just as Mary opened the refrigerator. "Hey, do you wanna go out to dinner?"

Mary closed the refrigerator. "Sure, that would be nice. Did you know Johnny was spending the night at Mike's?"

Bill spread his fingers around Mary's head and kissed her. "He told me in the car."

A ray of moonlight pierced the bedroom drapes and lit Mary's bare breast as Bill lay on top of her. He pulled his head forward to kiss Mary's neck, and then gently kissed each eyelid. "Have I told you that I love you?"

"I love you too," Mary whispered into his ear.

CHAPTER 23

Friday

Irene slowly smelled the bottle of Eau Dynamisante perfume, then dabbed it down the cleavage of her freshly showered body. She slipped her legs into black fishnet stockings before squeezing into her favorite leather black platform boots. She zipped up the denim skirt that she had ripped and bleached herself. She wore a low-cut, tight, white tank top and a vintage velveteen purple jacket.

She waited at an outside table at Starbuck's until Bill drove up in his red 1968 El Camino. The passenger door creaked when he pushed it open, and he yelled, "Get in."

Irene hopped in and said, "I love it! I've only seen one of these, in *American Graffiti*."

"That's my favorite movie," Bill said. "Slam the door hard. You wouldn't believe that this was a piece of shit when I bought it." Bill handed Irene a California driver's license. "Here's your ID."

Irene looked at the license for a twenty-two-year-old Melissa G. Wight and said, "She does look a lot like me. How did you get it so fast?"

"A customer at the bar can get me almost anything," Bill said, as he cautiously placed his hand on Irene's leg.

Irene looked at Bill's hand, took a joint out of her purse, lit it and took a hit. "Do you want some?"

Bill hadn't smoked pot since he'd married Mary eight years ago. "Sure." Bill took the joint, inhaled, and coughed.

Irene said, "Are you not used to smoking pot?"

"It's been a very long time." Bill took another smaller hit and seemed OK.

Bill placed his hand lightly back on Irene's leg and slowly moved it up until it was past her fishnet stockings and under her skirt.

As he touched her thong, Irene pushed his hand away. "How much longer to the club?"

Bill slowly took his hand off her panties but slid his hand between her legs, stroking her thigh, slowly removing his hand from under her skirt.

The Make Out Room was packed. A support pillar at the edge of the dance floor had a countertop ledge surrounding it. It held Bill's bottle of Gordon Biersch and Irene's martini as they danced on the floor. Irene shook her raised arms back and forward in unison with her pulsating hips as she rubbed up against Bill's body to Milton Mapes playing "There's a thousand songs about California." Bill thrust his waist against Irene, mimicking dirty dancing moves. They had three drinks each over the next hour and a half. The dancing quickly burned off the buzz. Bill wrapped his arms around her, pulled her body to his, and kissed Irene.

Irene said, "Do you want to get out of here?"

Once they arrived at the motel room, Irene looked in her purse and said, "Shit, I thought I had another joint." Bill reached into the nightstand, unrolled his sock and took out a joint and lit it. Bill and Irene passed it back and forth until it was only a short stub. Irene launched herself at Bill. Bill pulled the shoulders of her jacket down and started to unbutton her blouse.

Irene pulled at Bill's shirt, buttons popping off in her rush. Bill pushed her onto the bed and unzipped her skirt and pulled it off. Irene carefully slid off her fishnet nylons and then unbuckled Bill's pants. Bill ran his hands up and down Irene's young, naked body. He kissed her and laid her on the bed, circling his finger around her pink nipples. He pulled his head forward to kiss Irene's neck, and then gently kissed each eyelid. He entered her and was so excited he came in seconds.

"That's OK; just kiss me," Irene said.

Bill slowly caressed her body, moving down until he was between her legs. He gently licked her as her body became tense. Bill slowed down. Soon Irene was pulsing up and down. She grabbed his back with her nails and screamed as she climaxed.

They lay side by side, enjoying the calmness. Irene reached for another joint, which they both smoked.

She pushed Bill over and started to stroke him while he was on his back. To his surprise, he got another erection. It had been years since he ever was able to get a second one. Irene mounted him and put his penis inside her. She bounced up and down. Bill was able to stay erect for what seemed like half an hour. The passion built like he had never felt before. The pot was amplifying the sensation. The high was fantastic until he had a climax like he had never had before. He couldn't believe the deep, passionate feelings he experienced. Irene was sitting up with Bill still inside her. Bill just looked at her beautiful body.

"That was fun," Irene said with great excitement. "You are such a great writer. You have to get *Space Key* published."

Bill had never had anyone think he was important or smart. She made him feel special and he was starting to believe that he was an author.

"Let's go swimming," Irene said.

"Now?" Bill wasn't very excited. "We don't have swimsuits."

"We have our underwear." Irene was already out of the bed, putting on her bra and panties. She grabbed two bath towels from the bathroom. "Let's go!"

Bill put on his boxers, wrapped a towel around him, and followed Irene past the office to the pool in front of the motel. He opened the rusted cyclone gate that creaked loudly. Irene took off her bra and panties and jumped into the pool naked. Bill looked around to see if anyone was watching. The pool was in full view of the office and anyone walking on Taaffe Street. He pulled down his boxers and set it within reach of the pool and climbed down the stairs into the pool. Irene started splashing him while he was getting in. He swam to her and dunked her head under the water. They horse played a while until Irene started rubbing Bill's penis. Bill looked around nervously until he was sure nobody was watching. Soon he had an erection.

Irene pulled him until she was sitting on the bottom step. She wrapped her legs around Bill and guided his penis into her. As Bill pushed his penis in and out of Irene as she moaned, "Oh, oh, oh…," as if she didn't care if anyone heard. Bill focused on Irene's breasts, holding them while he continued having sex. The danger of being caught excited him. The excitement rose as he tilted his head back. He realized he was loudly making "Oh, Oh" shouts, and looked to see that they were alone.

In the morning, Bill woke up with Irene's arm across his chest. He gently rolled her onto her back and looked at her petite body. Irene opened her eyes and stared at Bill. He ran his hand over her breast, across her hips, and between her legs. Irene spread her legs for him. They stayed in bed until noon.

CHAPTER 24

December 22, 1992

John was in Sunnyside Assisted Living Center; his liver was failing from AIDS and alcohol, the doctor told him and he didn't have much time left. Bill and Colleen sat near his bed.

"I'm so happy you came to see me. This is wonderful."

Bill took a flask of Jameson out of his pocket and poured John a drink.

Colleen said, "John shouldn't be drinking!"

Bill handed the glass to John. "At this point, why can't he be happy?"

"Thank you, Bill." John took a sip, looked at the glass and took another drink from it. "Do you remember when your mother brought you to the bar? You were only thirteen and were a pissed-off brat. You wouldn't even call me Uncle."

"I know; I didn't want to leave my friends in San Francisco and then you forced me to do homework in the bar every day. Looking back, I don't know where I would be without you. Maybe in the jungle dead with Anthony."

John finished the glass. "I hate that I am in pajamas when you come."

"Uncle John," Colleen said, "we all love you and I don't care what you are wearing."

They visited for an hour before John became tired. Ignacio walked in and patted Bill on the back. "Hey, Bill, can you cover the bar for me?"

"Of course, Ignacio. He is in good spirits and enjoyed seeing us."

"Your uncle is like a puppy, always excited to see people."

"I know. Uncle John is the happiest person I know. Can we take him out of here for a few hours?"

"Sure." Ignacio said. "What do you have in mind?"

"Just bring him to the bar tomorrow about five."

Bill spent the rest of the day and the following morning calling all of John's friends and making arrangements.

The next afternoon, Ignacio helped John get into the car. "I'm just taking you for a ride. I think it will be good for you to get out of Sunnyside for a while."

"Thanks, Ignacio. This is nice."

Ignacio held onto a bank bag. "I need to drop this off at the bar for Bill. Why don't you come in."

"Not in my pajamas," John said.

Ignacio walked around the car and opened the door. "Oh, come on. Charlie and Bill will be happy to see you. We will just be a minute."

Ignacio pushed John's wheelchair into the bar. The bar was packed: Bill, Colleen, Charlie, Little Pat Riley, Mike, Florence, Angela, and twenty more friends were all dressed in pajamas.

"Surprise!" they all shouted.

Bill was dressed in a sexy black negligee and bunny slippers, and wore John's Marilyn Monroe blond wig. "It's a pajama party for you."

Colleen hugged John. "I couldn't get Bill to wear normal PJs."

"You guys all came here for me? I'm so lucky to have friends like you."

El Faro's catered the party. John was thrilled as he was tired of Sunnyside's food. "This is so good!" He ate two enchilada specials and downed quite a few Jamesons.

Everyone had a memory to share. "John was mad at me because I voted for Jimmy Carter." Charlie said. "To get even, he sent a huge balloon tied to a bouquet of red roses to my office. He wrote '**Charlie, Marry Me, Bruce**' on the balloon. Everyone in the office saw it and was convinced I was gay. I didn't live that down for years."

Florence said, "That explains a lot."

The party broke up at about ten as John was exhausted and drunk. Bill drove down a deserted El Camino Real. At the traffic light, he daydreamed, looking at Olson's Cherry Orchard; most the trees were rotted and falling down now. When he first came to Sunnyvale, there were still many huge orchards. He fondly remembered running though the rows of trees. With each stride, he floated high among the branches and grabbed a cherry for an instant treat.

Honk, honk, honk!

Bill's eyes sprung wide open to see the light was green and his car rolling toward the curb. He pulled over and watched the car behind pass by and turned at the light and pulled into Denny's. Tired, he had spent the last twenty-four hours arranging the party and had tended bar for the event. With no sleep and not eating much and having to pour so many drinks, he had to stop. It was the only place close by still open to eat, three days before Christmas at ten p.m.

Walking across the parking lot, there was an oxidized red, dented 1968 El Camino with a For Sale sign in the window. What a cool car, Bill thought, and wrote the phone number on his hand with a BIC® pen. He walked into the bathroom and looked into the mirror to see his straggly whiskers and rumpled shirt. He couldn't believe it and was uncomfortable being seen so unkempt. Washing his face in the basin and combing his hair made him more presentable. He looked down and realized he still had the bunny slippers on.

Inside, there was an older couple at a table and at the counter each end was taken. Bill took a seat in the middle of the counter. Two stools over, a fat, dirty biker at least two hundred pounds and over six feet tall flipped the lid back and forth of a Zippo lighter with a marijuana leaf insignia on it. A black widow spider tattoo radiated from his thick neck up to the top of his bald head. A Hell's Angel insignia was on the back of his black jacket.

Only one waitress was working. Her starched white skirt swooshed as she rushed up with a tray balanced above her head with her left hand and a coffee pot in her right. "Would you like coffee?" she stuttered.

Bill nodded his head. He was amazed with the circus act this stuttering waif performed with an overflowing tray of plates.

"I'll be right back."

Bill, mesmerized, turned and watched. Her petite body was covered in freckles, bright red hair exploded in curls from under a neckerchief tied in a triangle on the top of her head. She rushed off to a table with the elderly couple, set the tray down, and served their plates.

"Hey! Wawawawa… what gives?" the bald biker mimicked her stutter. "I was here before them. Where's my food?" He unzipped his black motorcycle jacket and looked at Bill and said, "Talk about shitty service." When Bill turned and nodded his head to acknowl-

edge the comment, he smelled the stale beer and cigarettes on the biker.

Bill looked back to check out this cute waitress,
who turned and caught Bill's blue eyes staring at her.
They were both embarrassed and looked away. She
hustled back and, holding the tray under her arm,
refilled the bald man's cup, and said, "I'll go back and
check on it," as she continued toward the kitchen.

"What does it take to get a-a-a-a... an order of
food here?" he shouted as she passed.

"It will be right up," she said as she turned to Bill
and asked, "What will it be?"

Bill was distracted by the asshole biker and hadn't
had time to look at the menu. Startled, he said, "Ah...
a... a... steak sandwich, fries, and a beer." He blushed
embarrassedly and hoped she didn't think he was making fun of her stutter.

She left and returned with an order and placed it
on the counter in front of the biker.

"What the fuck is this?" He poked the steak with
his fork. "It-it-it's... fuckin' burnt and I wanted grilled
onions." He got up and walked around to the counter,
holding the plate in his hand. "I'm gonna shove this in
the cook's face myself!"

She reached out to take the plate. "I'll ta-a-a...
take it for you."

He pulled the plate back and pinned her against
the wall with his hand in her face. "Don't you try to
stop me."

She was terrified. Her body trembled and she
dropped the metal serving platter, breaking all the

plates, which made a loud crashing sound. Anxiety and tremors took over her body. Her right arm flew uncontrolled above her head, trembling, as she said, "I'll see-e-e-e-e-e if if if your—" She couldn't continue and started to hyperventilate.

Bill looked in her eyes and relived the terror he felt when his father had slammed him against the bathroom door and twisted his hair until he cried.

Her body trembled as she tried to push him away but he just pinned her tighter. The old man at the table hurried over to the pay phone and dialed 911.

Bill grabbed the biker by his collar and pulled him back. "Hey asshole, do you like picking on girls? "

The biker looked down at Bill's slippers, "Fuck off or I will kick your ass too, you fuckin' fag!"

Bill had been well taught by Uncle John how to defend himself. He took a step back and raised his fist and said, "You'll go down as fast as the fat boy in dodge ball."

"This will be fun; I ain't never beat the shit out of a fag in bunny slippers." The man swung.

Bill effortlessly turned his body and deflected the punch with his right hand and he threw three rapid jabs into the man's face with his left hand. The biker fell back against the counter, knocking a plate to the floor, but he wasn't hurt. He has been in many a bar fight, Bill thought. "Hey asshole, I am not a homosexual and I like my slippers."

The biker charged Bill, swinging wildly. Bill dipped and dodged, waiting for an opening. As he ducked under a right punch, Bill started a quick series of left jabs to his face, followed by a hard right hand blow, throwing the biker up against the counter. While off balance, Bill landed a few more punches. Bill was excited, hands ready for another round. The biker stood motionless against the counter, bleeding from the nose.

"I think I'm leaving now."

As the biker started to walk away, Bill said, "What about the bill?"

The man looked at the order tag and set three dollars and two quarters on the counter.

Bill said, "I don't see a tip." He opened his wallet as Bill continued, "And it better be the biggest tip she's ever gotten."

The man put another three dollars on the counter and walked toward the door. "I'm calling the cops."

Bill remembered Uncle John's line and repeated it: "If Officer O'Reilly picks up the call, remind him to tell Chief Murphy that the poker game is at my place this week."

Bill stood there feeling his heart pounding, awake and feeling a rush of adrenaline. He had pictured in his mind many times stepping in to save a maiden in distress. He never thought he would ever have the courage or opportunity to do it.

The waitress's right hand trembled uncontrollably over her head as she reached down trying to pick the plate off the floor.

Bill was breathing hard. "Here, let me help you with this."

She couldn't speak, and her right arm still jerked.

Bill made her sit down and poured her a glass of water.

"I'll pick this up for you."

She finally sat on her right hand, holding it still. "No, you saved me… you need to *ga… go* before the po… po… police come. I can smell some beer on you."

Bill smiled. "Don't worry about it. I know every cop in Sunnyvale. Besides, I tended bar for most of them this afternoon"

"I'm Mary," she stuttered. "I don't know how to thank you."

He straightened his shirt. "Ah, it's not a big thing. I kind of enjoyed kicking that fat asshole's butt. It got my spirits up. I am tired and nothing is going well for me now." Bill sat down at the counter.

"Weren't you scared?" Mary asked. "He was so scary."

"Of him?" Bill pulled his shoulders back. "He had more chins then the Chinese phone book." Bill took a sip of his coffee. "Merry Christmas."

Mary sat the broken plate on the counter and they both started to laugh. "You're a funny guy. Merry Christmas to you, too." The humor seemed to help her get control of the anxiety that overwhelmed her.

Bill reached out to touch her hand and she instinctively pulled away. He said, "Take some deep breaths. All the way from your stomach; it will help calm you down."

"How do you know about this?" Mary said between deep breaths.

"I understand; my father used to beat the shit out of me," Bill said. "Just try to relax, breathe and think about being at your favorite place."

Officer Tim walked in with his hand on his gun holster. Bill explained that a drunken biker was roughing up the waitress so he had kicked him out. The elderly couple confirmed his story, saying how brave he was. They talked for ten minutes about John's party.

Bill said, "He had a great time. I'm glad we were able to make him so happy." They shook hands before he left.

Bill talked to Mary as she worked. "Do you have plans after you're off?"

"No," Mary said, "but everything's closed."

Bill smiled. "I got the keys to the bar where I work. We can go there."

"I don't drink," Mary said.

"That's OK. We can just talk."

Mary's stutter increased, "Thank you for saving me, but... but... I don't go out with men."

"That's OK. It's just... you are the first woman I have ever been this comfortable talking to. I was hoping we could spend some time together."

"I'm comfortable with you too." As Mary walked off to serve another order, she looked back to Bill.

He took another drink of his beer and waited until she came back with his steak sandwich. "What days do you work?"

Mary just looked at Bill while holding an empty tray. "I get off in an hour. You need to promise not to touch me unless I say it's OK."

"I promise. I would never hurt you."

The soft glow in Kelly's Bar came from the fluorescent Anchor Steam Beer sign above the glass shelves behind the bar. Bill led Mary to the back booth and turned the jukebox volume to low. The smell of left-over burritos was still in the air. He took two ice-covered martini glasses out of the freezer and filled his with gin and put sparkling water in Mary's.

"Thank you," Mary stuttered.

"My Uncle John taught me how to make it. Pretty damn good, yes?" Bill waited for Mary's approval.

Mary examined the glass and took a sip. "Yes, it's wonderful. Why did you become a bartender?"

"This is my uncle's bar. Growing up, I was always shy, but when I was old enough, Ignacio, his partner, let me bartend. I love being a bartender. It takes me out of my shell. I can be the popular guy, making jokes and playing the tough guy."

Mary said, "Just like you did tonight?"

"Well, yeah." Bill blushed. "You figured that out pretty quick. Besides, I didn't appreciate his fag comments. I have a lot of gay friends."

Bill wanted to run his fingers into her hair but stopped inches away. "I love your hair."

Mary smiled and turned her face away. "I hate it. I can't do anything with it. It's just wild curls. I would have given almost anything to have had normal hair growing up."

"I've always loved red hair. I think it's beautiful."

"Why were you in Denny's?" Mary asked.

"My Uncle John doesn't have long to live. I threw a party for him here. I was tired and hungry after."

"Oh, I'm sorry."

"He has always taken care of me and I have always been a total screw-up."

"I think you are being too hard on yourself. I bet he is proud of you."

Bill said, "Why don't you have anywhere to go tonight?"

Mary's eyes filled with tears. "I lost my mother last year on Christmas Eve. That is partly why I agreed to come out with you. I didn't want to be by myself."

"I'm sorry." Bill wiped her tears with a bar napkin. "How did she die?"

"My father strangled her." Tears rolled down her red checks. "If I was there, I might have been able to stop him."

Bill attempted to wrap his arms around her, but she pushed him away. "I'm sorry."

Mary said, "I've always been afraid to let a man touch me."

Instead, Bill put her two hands between his. "I won't hurt you. My father used to beat the crap out of me."

Mary allowed Bill to sit with their bodies leaning against each other.

Bill said, "Don't blame yourself—he might have killed both of you. I know how evil an abusive father can be. What happened to him?"

"He's in jail, but his trial starts in a month. I hope they give him the death penalty after what he did to her, and me." Mary held Bill's hands tight. "I never told anyone that before, but somehow I think you understand."

"When my father wanted to take us to the Peoples Temple, my mother took me and ran away to my uncle's. Six months later, we heard that they committed mass suicide. I prayed that he was dead. It was two weeks before we were notified. I felt guilty for wishing him dead but I felt relief in knowing he could never bother us again."

Two hours later, Bill gently touched Mary's face.

Her body stiffened "I didn't think I would ever let a man touch me."

Bill took his hand away.

Mary relaxed and moved closer. Bill lightly put his hand under her chin, turned her face toward him, and lightly kissed her.

"I have never been kissed before. It feels warm, like holding a puppy."

Bill had dated a few women from the bar but it never lasted. They were attracted to him because they were drinking and because of the energy at the bar. Once he was alone with a girl, his shyness would come out. He just wasn't the same guy they knew at the bar. "I have been with a couple of women but it never felt natural. That kiss was wonderful for me too."

Bill leaned over and kissed Mary again. Mary at first was motionless but quickly found herself with her arms around Bill.

Bill started to explore Mary's body.

Mary pushed his hand away.

"I promise I won't hurt you. If you say stop, I will."

"It's not you," Mary said. "It's just I have always been afraid of men."

"You have good reason to be afraid. I want to kiss you and feel you. If you say stop, I promise I will."

Bill gently turned her face and gave her a short, gentle kiss and pulled away.

Mary didn't push away. "I liked that. I have always been angry with my father because he destroyed any chance that I could have a relationship with any man."

Mary moved her face forward and initiated the next kiss.

"That was wonderful." Bill said.

The jukebox started playing, with Paula Abdul singing, "Rush, rush."

They talked again for another hour. Bill embraced her with both arms and kissed her again. He softly ran his fingers up her leg, just barely glancing over her skin.

Mary arched up, enjoying the tickling sensation from Bill's fingers.

Bill could see the enjoyment of the sensation in Mary's face. He pulled his hand away and let it slowly slide up under her blouse until he was gently feeling her nipples.

Mary was not resisting his advances, so he took his shirt off and took her hand and ran it up over his chest hair. Mary was excited and curious about Bill's body as she ran her hand through his chest hair. Bill kissed Mary and then unzipped his jeans, pulling them down to let Mary see his erect penis. Mary at first pulled away.

Bill said to her, "It's OK if you are not ready. I know you must be feeling a lot of fear from your past. We can stop now and go home."

Mary's fears melted away, and she took hold of Bill's penis. "I've never touched one before; it's so hard."

Bill slowly unbuttoned her blouse. He reached behind her to unhook her bra but struggled with it. Finally, Mary reached behind herself and unhooked it in two seconds. Bill felt her breast as he ran his hands up and down her torso until he finally felt confident enough to put his hands on her skirt. The skirt had a large pocket that Mary put her tips into directly above a button and zipper on her waist. Bill struggled to undo the button and then pulled the zipper down.

Mary didn't move.

Bill looked down at Mary's body as he stroked her with his hand and said, "Do you have any quarters in your tip pocket? There is a condom machine in the bathroom."

Bill hustled his naked body with his huge erection down the hall.

Mary could hear the handle of the condom machine each time he put a quarter into it. He turned it three times.

Bill returned, still erect, opened the first condom and put it on the tip of his penis; he took Mary's hand and helped her roll it down.

Bill lay on top of Mary, trying not to fall off the booth seat. His elbow stuck Mary in her ribs. She pulled back. "I'm sorry. Did I hurt you?" he asked.

"No, just trying to get comfortable. I can't believe I'm having sex with you in the back of a bar with rubbers from the bathroom condom machine."

"I'll try to be more careful."

Bill came within seconds of penetrating her. "I'm sorry; I didn't mean for it to happen so quickly."

They held each other, each embarrassed by the experience. They talked about their jobs and what movies they liked. Bill showed Mary the newspaper story of his Uncle John winning his only professional fight. "That is how he got the money to open this bar back in 1933."

Finally Mary said, "Was the sex good for you?"

"Sure, but I came too fast. Did you like it?"

"I didn't know what to expect. I have never had sex before. It hurt some but I liked having you inside me. Is it OK if I touch it?" She reached down and held his penis. It slowly stiffened as Mary lightly stroked it. "I didn't know it could grow so fast."

Bill unwrapped another condom. Mary rolled it down like an old pro. Bill got on top of her. He kissed her and their mouths sucked at each other's tongues.

Bill, trying to be gentle, entered her and they rolled simultaneously for what seemed like an hour before Bill came. Bill moved down Mary's body, gently kissing every part. Mary's body started to pulsate as she hyperventilated. The climax startled her as she screamed. She lay back.

"That was wonderful"

They held each other motionlessly until they both fell asleep.

★★★

Early Christmas Eve, Bill, still unshaven, arrived back at the nursing home wearing the same blue jeans and black sweatshirt from the day before. It was dark and a light rain fell as he searched the car's trunk for John's Christmas card and present. The squish of wet bunny slippers broke the quiet of the almost-deserted hallway. John's bed was empty. Ignacio and Colleen sat in the room.

"Hi, Mom. Where is Uncle John?"

Ignacio said, "He went into a coma last night and died just a few hours ago."

"I should have been here for him." Bill could only think about having sex when John needed him.

"Don't feel guilty, Bill." Colleen gave him a big hug. "You gave him the happiest day he has had in years. I'm just happy you gave him that party when you did."

CHAPTER 25

September 5, 2000

Bill arrived early at Joe Black's office. "Hello, Vicky; you look very nice today."

Vicky wore a halter top and black mini skirt. She rolled her eyes and stuttered, "Mr. Black should be in any time; have a seat."

"Thank you, Vicky; I hope I am not disturbing you."

"No, just have a seat," Vicky tried to pretend that she was busy typing a letter until Joe arrived.

"Well, Bill, I think you could have a best seller here. I did a little research and you are right that no publisher will give you the time of day.

Bill took a deep breath and sat up straight. "Thank you, Mr. Black."

"Call me Joe. You would make a good attorney if you wanted to give up writing. Your plan could work."

"Then you will take my case?"

"No." Joe stood up and paced across the room with the manuscript rolled up in his right hand. "You are just an ordinary husband who wants a divorce. Who cares?"

Bill slumped in his chair. "I don't understand."

"Mary has a much more interesting case. She is claiming community property rights to your future royalties for what you wrote! That could establish a legal precedent."

"Why won't you represent me?"

"Because if I am going to go out on a limb, I want something out of it. I want to win! You don't get it, because you need to file for divorce. I am not a divorce attorney." As Joe paced, he slapped the rolled-up manuscript against his left palm. "You cannot let on to the other attorney that this is just an attempt for publicity or they won't take the case. It would be unethical for an attorney to represent you and file a divorce proceeding if they knew you were just using the courts for publicity. You need to proceed as if you really want a divorce. Have you moved out of your house yet?"

"Yes, I moved into a motel a couple of days ago."

"Great!" Joe leaned forward and talked softly to Bill as if he were telling him a secret. "I know just who you need to use. You make an appointment with Darleen Lynch. She is the toughest divorce attorney in the county, a real shark."

Bill sat there with his mouth open, clenching a pencil in his hand. "Why do you want me to use a really tough attorney?"

"Because," Joe said, "she will put on a great fight. Some rookie would be afraid of going to court and try to settle. That won't help me. We need someone who isn't afraid to try cases and will use the press to advance her cause. Darleen will put up a great fight. She might even beat me, but the point is, you will be in the news. I see this case gaining national attention."

Bill started tapping the pencil on the desk. "I don't know this attorney. What happens if she doesn't want to take the case?"

"She is in this for the money," Joe said. "If you can pay her retainer, she will take the case. However, you cannot let her know that this is not an actual divorce case. If she thinks you are using her, she will walk away. We need her as she can gain the attention of the press. After you file for divorce, I will file an action against you for Mary's rights to your novel. This will get you what you want: national attention. I will have a news conference. The papers and news channels will probably print parts of your novel.

Bill was thinking everything was going as he planned until Joe said, "Remember, if Darleen even suspects that you are using her, she will drop the case. You need to convince her that you want this divorce."

CHAPTER 26

That Sunday, Bill, Mary, and Johnny were on their way to the see *Pirates of the Caribbean*. Mary sang "Five Little Monkeys" to Johnny in the car.

Johnny said, "Mom, that is a little kid's song. I just want to see the movie." Johnny wore a Jack Sparrow T-shirt and a Giants baseball cap. Bill gave the cashier three re-entry passes and she printed out tickets for them. Once inside, Bill told Mary to go find a seat and gave Johnny $10 to buy some popcorn. They were about fifteen minutes early, so Bill walked around looking at the posters advertising the upcoming movies. After five minutes, he paced by the front lobby door looking at his watch. He pulled his cell phone from his pocket and held it to his ear. Afterwards, he went up to the counter and said to the girl serving drinks and popcorn, "I just bought these tickets for me and my family but my wife just called me as my son just smashed his hand in the car door. She is taking him to the emergency room right now. Can I get a rain check to see the movie another day? Johnny will be so disappointed if he can't come back."

The cashier's blond ponytail bounced around as she talked quickly, "Oh, your poor boy. I hope he will be all right."

Bill held the tickets out. "I hope so too. I am going to the emergency room now. Little boys are always doing something."

"I can print you out three re-entry passes and you can come back anytime."

Bill thanked her, turned, and walked into the crowd. He waited until he was sure she wouldn't see him go back into the movie theater. He proudly showed Mary and Johnny the passes as he sat down next to Mary.

Johnny with popcorn in his mouth said, "How did you do that, Dad?"

"All you need to do to get what you want is to act convincingly. Most people want to help others."

Mary shook her head. "Bill, you are not setting a good example for Johnny. We should be teaching him to be honest."

"They don't care," Bill said. "The ticket prices are outrageous and the theater really makes their money on the concessions."

Bill reached over Mary for popcorn on Johnny's lap and flipped the brim of Johnny's cap with a finger, knocking it off.

"Dad, that's my Giants cap."

As he pulled a handful of popcorn from the cup, Bill said, "You need to be quicker."

Johnny flipped an un-popped kernel at his Dad. "You need to be quicker, Dad."

Mary said, "OK, that's enough. You would think I have two children."

After the movie, they all went for ice cream. Bill told Johnny that he was going to be gone for a job but it would be only for a few weeks.

Johnny started to cry. "Why can't you stay, Dad?"

Mary put her hands on her hips. "I told you Johnny would be upset."

Before Mary could finish her sentence, Bill tossed his cone into the garbage. "God damn it! I told you this will only be for a couple of weeks. You need to go along with this." Bill left the store, leaving Johnny crying and Mary to walk the four blocks home.

CHAPTER 27

The next morning, Bill arrived at Darleen Lynch & Associates in the Alfred Alquist State Building across the street from San Pedro Square. The office occupied the two top floors and featured panoramic views of the valley. There was a rush of activity with associates, paralegals, secretaries, and the receptionist all busy with files.

Bored, Bill waited in an office, flipping the pages of *People* magazine. He was uncomfortable and kept readjusting his position.

A very young, thin, Asian girl dressed in a gray pin-striped suit walked in with a folder in her hand. "Hello. I'm Angela Ng." She reached out to shake Bill's hand. "I will be handling your case."

Bill was surprised how tight a grip Angela had when he held her handshake. "I thought Ms. Lynch would be taking my case." Bill was worried that this might screw up his plan. Angela looked young enough to still be in high school.

"Oh, don't worry. Darleen Lynch supervises each case the firm takes in."

Angela sat down behind the huge oak desk, which only emphasized her small size. "Tell me, Mr. Giovanni, what brings you here today?"

Bill felt nauseated. He cleared his throat. "I want a divorce."

"Well, Mr. Giovanni, you don't sound very convincing that this is what you really want."

Bill was caught off guard and worried he might get exposed by this little girl. He nervously jerked his hand and knocked the *People* magazine off the desk. His forehead dripped sweat as he reached down to pick it up and place it on the desk. "Yes, Ms. Ng, I want a divorce. That is why I am here."

"Are you seeing someone else?"

How could this girl see through me so quickly? This was the first time he was ever questioned about one of his scams and he was nervous. "I have met another woman, but this was after I moved out and we aren't serious."

"And how old is this woman, Mr. Giovanni?"

"She is young, Ms. Ng. She took an interest in my writing and we just felt a connection,"

"How young?" Angela asked.

"She is twenty-one," Bill lied. Irene was only nineteen, but Bill for the first time was self-conscious about their affair. He wiped his forehead with the back of his sleeve. "But she is very mature and is helping me edit my novel. I don't see what difference this makes!"

Angela picked up the questionnaire Bill had filled out and studied it for a couple of minutes. This was her fourth case, and they had all involved middle-aged men having affairs with a younger woman.

Bill leaned forward with both arms pressed on the desk. He looked into Angela's eyes and spoke tensely, "I have already separated from my wife and I am living at a weekly motel. It isn't that I hate her; it is just that we have become distant. My wife isn't interested in me anymore. It is as if we are only living together because we have a son."

"Tell me about you and your wife."

Bill thought for a moment as he felt his heartbeat normalize. "We have been married eight years and have a seven-year-old son."

"What property do you own?"

"I own our house. It is very old and in need of remodeling, but it is on Francis Street just a block from downtown. It was my mother's. I inherited Kelly's Bar, but my Uncle John put it in a trust. I have to lease it to Ignacio Rodriquez for one dollar a year for the rest of his life. My uncle wanted to take care of Ignacio as they had lived and worked together for years."

Angela's voice softened as she set the questionnaire down and directly looked at Bill. "Where do you and your wife work and how much do you make?"

"Mary works full-time at Space Key. She makes about seventy thousand a year and has the health benefits. I work part-time at my uncle's old bar for Ignacio. I only get paid about thirty thousand a year, but he pays me cash under the table to avoid taxes, and I get tips."

"Who takes care of your son?" Angela asked.

"We both take care of him, but I spend more time with him, working only part-time and mostly at night."

Angela wrote a few notes in the folder. "Well, your property isn't community property but since you moved out, you will never be able to regain possession of it. She could get a restraining order to keep you out."

Bill rested his chin on his hand. He felt as if he had regained control of the interview. "Mary and Johnny need a place to live. The house is very modest and if I have to allow them to stay there, I can live with that. I can stay in the motel for now. At your rates, I think it is smarter to let Mary live in the house rather than starting an expensive battle. I want Mary and Johnny to be happy. Besides, when I sell the book I wrote, I should be OK on funds."

"I didn't realize you are a published author," Angela said.

"Not yet," Bill responded, "But it is just a matter of time."

"When did you write this book?"

"I have been writing it over the last four years."

Angela thought for a moment. "I wouldn't try to get it published until after your divorce is final. After all, Mary was the breadwinner while you wrote this. Right now, you will be entitled to alimony and half of her 401k."

Bill sat back and relaxed in the overstuffed leather chair. "Good point. After four years of hard work, a few extra months to wait won't be difficult. When will Ms. Lynch get involved?"

Angela said, "She only gets directly involved if the case becomes complicated or needs to be litigated in court. Don't worry; if anything unusual comes up, she will be on top of this." She handed Bill a contract. "Sign the agreement and we will need a retainer for three thousand dollars." As Bill looked at the paperwork, she said, "We can have divorce papers filed by Wednesday if you want."

Bill took his checkbook out of his back pocket and said, "Yes, I appreciate that."

CHAPTER 28

Bill parked in front of the school in his El Camino later that afternoon. It was very hot; he had both windows down but there was no breeze to cool the car. When Johnny saw the car, he looked around to see if anyone was looking.

Don Callahan yelled at him, "What a piece of shit for a car, Johnny!"

Johnny ran as fast as he could to avoid anyone else making fun of him. He was already hot and sweaty and the run had him completely overheated. The door made a loud screeching sound when he opened it.

He looked at his father, ready to cry, when Bill said, "Do you want to go swimming, Johnny?"

All was instantly forgiven as they took off for the Hacienda Motel. Bill had brought their suits, which they changed into quickly. Johnny jumped into the shallow end as he couldn't swim. Bill splashed him and Johnny splashed him back. Bill started a game where they would take a breath and sit on the bottom to see who would last the longest. The first attempt, Johnny jumped right back up, but after a couple of times, he was able to stay under until he counted to ten.

Bill said, "If you can do this, you can swim."

He held Johnny in a floating position and glided him into the steps. Soon he had Johnny pulling his arms and within half an hour he was swimming twenty feet out to Bill. It wasn't long before Johnny was diving into the pool, swimming out to his father. Finally, Johnny was tired from swimming and wanted to get out. They both got out and dried off.

Bill asked, "Are you afraid of those boys at school?

"Yeah, Dad, they are always picking on me. Don Callahan steals my lunch money."

"I was picked on to when I was little. You Uncle John taught me how to box when I was thirteen. Nobody picked on me after that. Do you want me to teach you?"

"Your Uncle John knew how to box?"

"He sure did. Next time you are at Kelly's, I will show you the newspaper story about Uncle John winning a boxing match against a championship contender. That is how he got the money to build the bar."

Bill stood Johnny up and turned his body sideways. "OK, first, you need to keep your arms up like this. Stand sideways so you are a smaller target."

Johnny tried it.

"No, wrong side. You want to lead with your left hand. Keep it up, now jab at my hand quickly."

Johnny jabbed for about two minutes. "My arm is getting sore."

"That's because you haven't done this before. If you practice every day, your arm will get stronger. This will give you the advantage against Don. He might be bigger but I bet he won't be able to keep his arms up very long."

Johnny boxed with Bill for a while. "I think I am getting better, Dad."

"You are. I have a speed bag at the bar. I will bring it home tomorrow and set it up for you. If you use it every day for just ten minutes, nobody will pick on you ever."

At five-thirty, it was time to pick Mary up from work. When she got into the car at Space Key's parking lot, Johnny, in a very fast, excited voice said, "I can swim, Mom. I was diving out to Dad and swimming."

"That's great Johnny!"

"And Dad is teaching me to box."

Mary smiled. "I glad that you spent the afternoon with Johnny. Let's go to the Longhorn. I've been craving their steak sandwich."

The Longhorn was a Sunnyvale fixture, with a huge dining room furnished with old vinyl-covered booths that hadn't been changed in twenty-five years. Customers ordered at the counter and put on their own condiments at a counter on the side. Bill and Mary ordered steak sandwiches and beer while Johnny ordered a hotdog and milk shake.

After they started eating, Bill said, "On Wednesday, you will be served with papers." Mary's eyes welled up with tears, but before she could say anything, Bill continued, "You have an appointment with Joe Black on Thursday. We are going to make this quick. After we get some publicity, we can call off the divorce."

★★★

Thursday morning, Mary wore a pink flowered skirt as she walked quickly down Market Street past the Bad Boy's Bail Bonds and Jake's Bar. There were four Harley-Davidson bikes parked outside and three tattooed bikers smoking cigars in front of the door.

"Can I buy you a drink?" one of them yelled to her.

Mary walked faster and coughed from the smoke. She gave a sigh of relief when she arrived at Joe Black's office. Vicky stuttered, "Hello, I'm Vicky. Can I help you?"

Mary panicked as she stuttered back, "I'm-m-m… Mary G-G-Giovanni."

Both Mary and Vicky faces blushed with embarrassment. Mary stood quietly thinking for a minute and then sang in the tune for "Five Little Monkeys," "I am so sorry, I am Mary and I am singing. This is the only way I can keep from stuttering."

Vicky laughed. "I never thought about it, but I don't stutter when I sing either."

Vicky stood up, her miniskirt showing off her long legs and barely covering her rear. She gave Mary a seat while she waited.

Now I know why Bill came here, Mary thought.

Vicky led Mary into Joe's back office.

Mary stuttered, "M–My husband Bill told me to bring you these papers." She handed the divorce complaint to Joe and sat in the black leather chair.

"Thank you." Joe took a moment to look at Mary in her flowered skirt, bright red curly hair, and freckled face. Joe took the papers and examined them silently for five minutes. He looked back up and thought, God, she is beautiful.

Mary sat in the chair in front of the desk and watched a fly buzzing against the window as she chewed her fingernail.

"Take it easy, Mrs. Giovanni. This will be easy and I will do all the work."

Mary stuttered, "Bill has gone over the edge with this scam of his. We are going to get caught."

Joe stood up and paced back and forth behind his desk as he explained what he was going to do. "I will file a response to this petition tomorrow. Bill has asked for support, half of your retirement, and joint custody of Johnny. We are going to ask that his novel be introduced into evidence and counterclaim that you should receive fifty percent of the royalties. Afterwards, I will call a press conference. With my reputation, there will be a lot of attention."

Joe sat back down and focused on Mary. He reminded himself that he needed to be professional as he was attracted to Mary. "We can make this work. I want the press to fall in love with you and make you their favorite story."

"I don't understand what you want me to do."

"You don't need to do anything except be beautiful. I will call a press conference and give the reporters excerpts from the book. You just need to stand by my side." Joe asked Mary to stand up while he carefully examined her.

Joe Black was notorious for representing the more ill-reputed characters in the county. Two months ago, he got Frank "The Fix" Martinez's case for being San Jose's largest meth supplier dismissed. First, he leaked rumors about the crime lab losing drugs to a couple of addict employees. He then got a grand jury to investigate and they confirmed some evidence was being siphoned off for personal use. Employees were named and charged. Joe used this to question the integrity of the evidence. The judge agreed and threw out the entire case.

When Joe Black called a press conference, the media attended. This press conference was announced by his staff to all the major news outlets as being a groundbreaker. He arranged for it to happen on the county courthouse steps at two p.m. on a Wednesday afternoon, as he knew this was the slowest news day of the week and he would gain maximum exposure.

Mary was nervous about being inspected. Finally, Joe said, "I know what we need to do. I will take you to Eastridge and buy you the right dress. Appearance is everything."

Mary straightened out her dress. "I don't want to be a bother."

"Nonsense." Joe got up from behind his desk and approached Mary and held her hands. "I want you to look great for the press. After we shop, we can have lunch. Are you ready?" He had Mary wrap her hand around his arm as he led her out of the office. He turned to Vicky. " I will be out until later in the afternoon."

★★★

Wednesday afternoon there were four TV vans with their satellite dishes pointed skyward across the street. Reporters held a bouquet of foam-covered microphones, all with call letters: KGO, CBS, KNEW, CBS 5, and at least eight others. There was shoving as they all vied for position. Joe was milking the opportunity as he stood there with Mary and Johnny, holding her hand. She looked beautiful in a bright green spring dress, out-of-control red curls, and her freckled face. Mary looked shyly away from the cameras.

"Ladies and gentlemen of the press, I called this conference because of an injustice so huge that I am taking this case pro bono. My client, Mary Giovanni, has been supporting her husband for seven years while he has been writing an exposé of Space Key. Not only has she supported him, but all the content of the book has been supplied by her. Now her husband, Bill Giovanni, is divorcing her shortly before the novel is ready to be published. I will be petitioning the courts to make the novel community property. I personally have read the manuscript and I am convinced that it will be a huge commercial success with publishing contracts as well as movie rights. I think this case will be a landmark case deciding ownership of intellectual rights when parties divorce."

Reporters all started asking questions at the same time, making it impossible to distinguish them through the roar. Joe took control and pointed to Marsha Lowe of Channel 9 news. "I'll take Marsha's question first."

"Mr. Black, is your client suggesting that she is entitled to half of the rights for a book her husband created?"

Joe answered back, "That is exactly what we are claiming. He would have never been able to write this book without Mary Giovanni supporting him."

It was a little ironic that this Irish-looking woman had a Italian last name, which made the attraction even better. Joe pointed to Gary Clark of KGO radio. "Yes, Gary."

"Your client is the person that has an income. Should she be required to pay spousal support to her ex-husband?"

"That is the reason I took this case," Joe said. "Without good legal support, Mary would be required to pay her ex-husband. But that would be a huge injustice, as he has been a parasite able to live off her while he created a novel that could be worth a lifetime of royalties. I have excerpts of the novel for each of you."

That evening, Joe's interview was on the local TV news broadcast. *The Mercury News* carried the story the next day, with excerpts of the novel. It described software for the stealth submarine being leaked to the Chinese.

Mary began receiving phone calls from reporters as well as coworkers. Finally, she stopped at Walgreens and bought sleeping pills. When she finally arrived home, she unplugged the phone.

CHAPTER 29

Rodger was mentally prepared for his new assignment with Space Key. Steven Case had demoted him, but at least he would be off the submarine tracking project. His only regret was that he still needed to report to Steven Case. He wore wrinkled gray slacks and a pastel blue collared dress shirt. He sat down in a booth at Denny's and ordered their Grand Slam. He sipped his coffee while he opened the newspaper. The headline read "Wife sues hubby for Space Key novel." Underneath were excerpts from the book as well as detailed information about Bill and Mary.

"Holy shit!"

The waitress turned to see if anything was wrong, but Rodger's eyes were buried in the article in the paper. He read the interview twice and the excerpt from the novel over and over. When his pancakes came, he only ate a few bites, then got up and left ten dollars on the table. He called Steven Case to tell him he was sick and would be out for at least two days.

Steven asked if he had seen today's paper. Rodger said no, as he was sick in bed.

Rodger arrived at the county recorder's office at nine a.m. with a request for a copy of the divorce complaint with the twenty-five-dollar fee. He read the complaint and underlined the property listed by Bill. He immediately recognized the bar as the one where Paul had died. He drove to Bill's house on Francis Street, but nobody was home. He then went to Kelly's Bar, but it didn't open until 11:30. He had an hour to wait in his car. His hands were sweating and the underarms of his dress shirt were stained as well. It seemed like an eternity. When Kelly's Bar opened, he sat on a barstool and said, "Is Bill in?"

It was early and nobody else was in the bar yet. Bill looked at this geeky guy in slacks and dress shirt. "Who's asking?"

"My name is Rodger Hinds. I work at Space Key and I know who wrote the novel you are calling yours, and I can prove it."

Bill stood, staring at Rodger. "Go fuck off and get the hell out of here." Bill tried to look unconcerned, but he had the same feeling he had felt when Uncle John pretended to be turning him into the police for writing in the fresh concrete.

"OK, tough guy." Rodger was sweating. "Paul was my best friend. I have twenty years of his notebooks detailing everything that happened at Space Key."

"So what? Notebooks don't prove anything." Bill walked away and turned his back to arrange the bottles behind the bar. "Paul couldn't have worked there. He spent every afternoon here. Why do you care about this book?"

Rodger started tapping his fingers on the bar and thought, He isn't even frazzled. "Look, all I care about is that I am not incriminated in giving out any of the information. I could get fired."

Bill decided to hold onto the story Joe Black and he had decided on. "Paul was here every day. I have a number of customers that will confirm that. Paul wanted me to write a book. He hated Space Key."

"Look," Rodger said, "We both know you didn't write the book. All I want is any reference of me out of it. I don't think you would want any suspicion that you didn't write it. You would never get it published."

Bill was unusually quiet. Finally Rodger said, "I want the manuscript and the disc tomorrow. We can meet at Denny's."

Bill was violently wiping the bar down with a sponge when Ignacio came in with the *San Jose Mercury News* in hand. "What the fuck! I have to hear about you divorcing Mary in the newspaper!"

"It's not what it looks like, Ignacio. Mary and I are OK."

"Bullshit! Mary's a sweetheart and you are going to break her heart. And what about Johnny? Have you thought about what this will do to him?"

Bill set the sponge down and sat on a barstool with his face in his hand, not wanting to look at Ignacio. "Believe me, I am doing this to help Mary."

"And what's this about a novel about Space Key? I didn't ever see you writing."

"Ignacio, this is a legal matter and I can't tell you everything but if I'm divorcing Mary and I wrote the book, then she won't get fired."

"When you were thirteen and you and your mother showed up here, I knew you were a screw up. John wanted to help and I loved John and would never say no to him. I thought you would have grown up by now and stopped with all your schemes."

Just then Charlie sat at the bar. Bill grabbed a bottle of Jameson.

"Have you lost your mind?" Charlie asked. "Finding Mary was the best thing that ever happened to you. I still remember when you first brought her here. John had just passed and everyone was depressed until we saw you had someone special in your life."

"Charlie, it's not as it seems but I can't explain it yet."

"I read the article, and I figure it is just another of your get-rich-quick scams. Well, they never work and now you are going to hurt someone who loves you. You are an idiot."

Bill made Charlie an Old Fashion without saying a word. He didn't even make eye contact.

An hour later Ignacio said, "Bill, we have never been this packed since John ran the place."

A large man with a wrinkled, poorly fitting plaid sports jacket and a note pad in hand squeezed up to the crowded bar. "Hi… Bill?"

"Yeah, I'm Bill. What will you have?"

"I'm Allen Johnson from the *Merc*. I just want to ask you a couple of questions."

"Get the fuck out of here. I'm working and not going to talk to any reporter."

"This will just take a minuet."

"Out!"

Bill pulled Ignacio aside. "I have a lot going on. Can I have the rest of the day off?"

Bill felt awkward as they all thought Bill was being an asshole and divorcing Mary.

"Fuck no. I can't handle this crowd alone and it is all because of you that we are packed. When your uncle ran the place, people came here because he was a great man and everyone loved him. He is probably turning over in his grave at this obscenity against his legacy."

Bill was sweating, cringing every time a customer called his name or asked him a question. The bar was filled with customers he had never seen before. He jumped a little every time a stranger just asked for a drink. I am sure they are investigating me, he thought.

Ignacio was fighting to keep his eyes open and glared at Bill if he even had the nerve to look at him. It was a long night for both of them and at two Bill locked the door as Ignacio had left the mess to him.

Bill arrived at his house at two-thirty a.m. and shook Mary until she appeared awake, still in a stupor from the sleeping pills. "We're fucked!"

The day with attorneys and having to go in front of the press at the conference had proven to be too much for Mary. "Bill, what are you doing? I need to sleep." She rolled back over, but Bill wouldn't let her go back to sleep.

"Wake up, God damn it! We are screwed. Some geek from Space Key came into the bar today and told me he knows I didn't write the book. He wants to meet tomorrow at Denny's."

Mary closed her eyes and said, "This is your problem. Don't bother me until you know what he wants. I'm going back to sleep."

★★★

A cool mist filled the air with just enough moisture to slightly dampen the sidewalk. Bill walked deliberately so as not to slip. He held a large tan envelope when he walked into Denny's and instantly noticed the smell of waffles and syrup. It brought back memories from when Mary was a waitress there and he had spent almost every afternoon there just to be close to her. He spotted Rodger, wearing a plaid shirt and worn jeans, in a booth. As he sat down, a waitress asked if he wanted coffee.

Bill said, "Yes, and a short stack of pancakes."

After a long silence, Bill asked Rodger, "What do you want?"

Rodger tapped his finger on the table and quickly said, "Right now, I want a copy of the book. After I read it, I will let you know."

Bill handed him the envelope with a copy of *Space Key*. "After you tell me what you want, I will consider giving you the other copies."

Rodger flipped through the pages and said, "Oh shit," when he got to the chapter about the source codes for the stealth submarine programs. "Who else has a copy of this?"

Bill paused for a minute, "My wife and the attorneys. I have the rest of the copies. I haven't sent any copies to publishers yet."

Rodger took a deep breath, "Can you get all the copies back today?"

"Maybe, but what do you want?"

Rodger looked directly into Bill's eyes. "Did you really think you could pass this off as something you wrote?"

Bill picked up his coffee and took a slow sip. "Look, you have a lot more to lose than me. I can get the copies but I'm not giving them to you until I see what you intend to do. If you just want to hide your involvement and keep your mouth shut, I might even give you a tiny cut." Bill handed Rodger a copy of the disc.

Rodger clenched his fist. "We can meet tomorrow."

"OK, but not here." Bill thought for a moment. "Do you like beer?

"Yeah, beer is my favorite."

Bill put a five dollar bill on the table and said, "We can meet at Faultline on Oakmead; they have great beer. I'll see you there at three p.m." Bill walked away without letting Rodger have the time to reply.

★★★

Bill spent the rest of the morning reading more of *Space Key*. He recognized Rodger in the book immediately by his grease-stained shirt and his disdain for Steven Case, although his name in the book was Alex. Paul told of Rodger's love for Xing Juan and described the earthquake and how he slept with Xing Juan that night. Rodger became a follower of Falun Gong because of her. Bill had never heard of this cult and he was not satisfied with the limited information Paul gave in the book. Bill looked it up and couldn't believe he had never heard of this cult. Bill paid attention to news about every cult. After all, his father tried to take him to live at the Peoples Temple.

Rodger shared his hatred for Space Key, his role in developing military products, and especially how Steven Case had demoted him and made his contributions to developing their most successful software irrelevant. He described a little about Falun Gong with its millions of followers around the world. The U.S. Congress had just passed a resolution to support Falun Gong in retaliation to the Chinese government banning the practice. The Internet was full of blogs, gatherings, and chat sites. The teachings seemed benign, as they taught truthfulness.

There was a gathering in Sunnyvale, so Bill decided to go to Questa Park the next night. In his search, he found a *New York Times* report that Falun Gong followers had filed a lawsuit against Space Key for selling the Chinese government the Golden Wall firewall designed to censor the internet and to track opponents as well as identify followers of Falun Gong. Steven Case was directly named in the suit.

Bill was nervous. He didn't trust Rodger. He arrived at Darleen Lynch's office at four that afternoon. He asked for Angela, but she was out on a deposition. Darleen offered to see Bill in her office.

"Ms. Lynch, it is a pleasure to finally meet you. I came here because of the fantastic reputation you have."

"Well, thank you, Mr. Giovanni. What brings you in today?"

"I gave Ms. Ng a copy of the novel I'm writing and I found a couple of serious mistakes in the manuscript that I need to edit." He asked Darleen for the manuscript back and said he would have a corrected copy in a day. She didn't suspect anything and gave him the book. Bill was relieved that he didn't need to ask Angela Ng. She had grilled him at their first visit and saw through his lies.

Mary went to Joe Black's office and stuttered, "I need... t-the copy back. We found an error that we need to fix."

Joe stayed in his chair behind the desk. "I need to make copies for our press conference. I can't give it back to you now."

Mary's right arm flew over her head in a violent tremor as she barely got out, "You don't understand." Her stuttering became so intense that Joe didn't know if she would be able to finish what she was trying to say. "Bill p-put s-someone's name in the b-book... that will be hurt if we don't change it."

Joe said, "Mary, have a seat and try to calm down. I will give it back to you but I need it by Monday."

With her arm still trembling above, she stuttered, "Thank you, Mr. Black."

"That's OK, Mary." Joe gave Mary a hug, "Just try to calm down." Joe got up and pulled open a file drawer to get the manuscript out and handed it to Mary.

Mary put her hand on her chest and nodded her head as she retreated from the office. Once outside the office, Mary became completely relaxed as she skipped to her car. This was the first time she had faked an attack, and she thought, that worked perfectly.

That evening, Bill went to Questa Park. The western sky was bright orange from the sunset. The cooling air was refreshing after the hot, busy day. Bill sat on the crest of the lawn overlooking about thirty people ranging in age from their early twenties to mid-seventies, who were dressed in gold karate-like robes. The leader stood in front while the others followed his slow, deliberate circling stretching motions silently while in deep meditation. Bill thought it resembled a slow-motion kung fu exercise movie.

Rodger was also busy that evening. He went into Space Key at six p.m., explaining that he had been sick but had a deadline tomorrow for a project. Rodger put the disc in his computer and spent hours editing *Space Key* to incriminate Steven Case. He deleted most of the parts about Alex. He thought it was convenient that Bill's wife worked in the assembly room.

Around midnight, nobody was left in the building, so Rodger went to Steven Case's office. He had made a key a couple of years ago when Steven was at an all-day conference and had left his keys on his desk. Rodger took them during his lunch hour and had made copies of every one of Steven's keys.

Rodger opened Steven's computer, using Steven's grandchildren's names for the password, and worked for hours planting incriminating information. He created e-mails between him and Mary that appeared to be a couple of years old into Steven's archived e-mails. He also created e-mails to a local bookie. He made WikiLeaks a favorite website with backdated transmissions to it. He had old racing forms he had found at Paul's apartment. He circled long shots with $1,000 next to the horse. Finally, he put the disc that he had with the sabotaged software for the stealth submarine into his computer and downloaded its contents into a hidden folder. He then e-mailed that folder to Xing Juan dated two weeks before her murder in Hong Kong.

Bill was waiting for Rodger at Faultline at three o'clock, not sure if he would show up. One big-screen TV above the bar played the San Francisco Giants game. They were in the fifth inning, up three to one over the

Padres. Rodger walked in wearing blue jeans and the same wrinkled plaid shirt. He hadn't shaved, his hair was oily, and he had circles under his half-closed eyes. Bill waved to the waitress as Rodger sat down. "Give us a pitcher of Belgian Triple and an order of calamari, darling."

The waitress smiled and asked if they wanted water. Bill answered, "No."

"You are going to love this beer, Rodger. It is one of the best beers I have ever had." What Bill didn't tell Rodger was that he picked Faultline because Belgian Triple has ten percent alcohol content. "I first met Paul at a Falun Gong event at Questa Park. I am a huge fan of Falun Gong. I regularly go to their classes at Questa Park. Paul would come into my bar and ask me questions about it."

The waitress set the beer on the table and filled a glass for each of them. Rodger drank half the glass in his first swallow. Bill took a sip of his beer while Rodger finished off his glass. Rodger's face reddened and he sat back in his chair with his eyes wide open.

"I go there, too. I have been into Falun Gong for five years now. Xing Juan was a close friend of Li Hongzhi." Bill had no idea who Li Hongzhi was, but he assumed he had something to do with Falun Gong.

Bill played along, "Really? Did you ever meet him?"

"No, he has been under close watch by the Chinese government and they won't let anyone contact him."

Bill put his elbow on the table and rested his chin in his hand. Rodger stopped talking and just stared into his half-empty glass. Bill topped it off and refilled his glass with only two sips missing. "Once, I got Paul so drunk that he wouldn't stop talking about Space Key. It wasn't long before three of my customers who also work there joined in. I was pouring drinks for the whole bar, making mental notes of the conversation. I got off at two a.m. but couldn't go to sleep until I wrote everything I still remembered down in my notepad."

Rodger looked up from his beer. "I didn't realize you were such great friends. He never mentioned you to me."

What a sap Rodger is, Bill thought. He stared into Rodger's eyes. "That's odd, as he never mentioned you to me either.

Rodger finished his glass. Bill took another sip of his beer and quickly refilled Rodger's glass. This time, Rodger only took a sip. "Paul didn't work at Space Key. He called them a war monger. Paul and I were roommates all through college until he dropped out. I think he kept quiet about knowing both of us. He was talking about stuff he got from me, his thirty-year drinking buddy."

"You're right!" Bill tapped glasses with Rodger. "I can see why you were such great friends. I am really happy that we met."

"You know, I am, too." Rodger took another drink. "I completely misunderstood you. I just added some more detail about the management and removed some of the description of Alex." He joined Bill with his arm supporting his chin on the table. "How would you like to go to Questa Park next week?"

Bill nodded his head.

Rodger slurred his words, adding, "Falun Gong changed my life. I was happy making machines of destruction until Xing Juan introduced me to Falun Gong. We can only work for peace and I am contributing to the military. I hate it." Rodger went on for a half hour about the teachings of Falun Gong.

Bill relived his father, Anthony, saying the same words about Jim Jones. It amazed him that he was hearing the same voice. "The father will save us. We are all going to the Peoples Temple to free ourselves from this corrupt world." He let Rodger continue, even as his each and every word irritated him.

He finally interrupted Rodger. "I soon became the spot for Space Key employees to unwind. I was pouring a lot of free drinks just to get material for my writing. In about a year, I had the makings for the book." What a fuckin idiot this guy is, Bill mused. He is actually buying my bullshit. They finished the calamari. Bill waved his hand for the waitress. "Can we get another round of both?"

The waitress said, "Sure," and picked up the empty pitcher and calamari basket.

"You picked a great spot, Bill," Rodger said. "This is great beer."

"Thank you, Rodger. Now let's talk about what you want to do with the book."

"I am going to trust you. I printed out six copies of the book for you. I only made a few changes in order to protect mine and Paul's identity. You can use these to distribute."

Bill flipped through the pages quickly without noticing a significant difference. "I don't understand. Do you want me to go ahead and publish the book?"

"Damn right, I'm sure. Steven Case arranged for Xing Juan's murder and he rigged the submarine software to help the Chinese navy track our submarines. He is deeply in debt to a bookie and I think he did this for the money. This novel will expose Steven; you will be a hero."

Bill stared at an open copy of the manuscript for a minute before he said, "Thank you, Rodger. This will really help me."

Rodger was feeling the beer. "You aren't getting this for free. I want half of all the royalties, and you need to convince me that you're capable of getting a publisher."

Since Rodger could end up in jail, Bill decided he was in no position to dictate terms. "Bullshit. You can't blackmail me."

Rodger turned red with embarrassment for making such a threat. He had been practicing this offer before the meeting and assumed Paul wrote the book. He slumped in his chair and said, "I am sorry." He took another drink. "OK, just give me all the other copies so I don't have to worry about the original script getting out."

"Don't worry about it." Bill handed Rodger the other copies he had brought with him. He didn't mention that he still had the original disc and laptop. "We're friends now. I can get it published. I already have the newspapers carrying stories about the book. Our divorce is just a scam for publicity." Bill now started drinking at the same pace as Rodger. "I'll take care of you. If you help me with the details, I'll give you a small split. Remember, this will be tax-free money to you. You may be able to retire on it."

Rodger smiled. "Oh, shit, Bill. I think you got me drunk. We have a deal." Rodger reached his hand out and shook Bill's hand. They finished the third pitcher of Belgian Triple and decided to call a cab to drive them both home.

CHAPTER 30

The Superior Courtroom of Judge O'Day was paneled in dark oak. A rail separated six rows of seating from the inner court. Judge O'Day's desk sat high on a podium where he presided over the plaintiff tables in front of him. Darleen Lynch wore a long gray skirt, a white blouse, and a gray blazer. She sat in court between Bill and Angela Ng. She leaned over and whispered to Angela, "Why the hell is Joe Black taking a divorce case?"

Joe Black sat next to Mary. Her white cotton dress showed her curves and cleavage. Her red ringlets touched her shoulders. Joe wore a double-breasted dark pinstriped suit, gold cufflinks, and a bright red bowtie. He looked as if he'd just walked out of a 1920s nightclub.

"Your Honor," he started, "it may appear on paper that Mary makes more money, but Bill has deferred income coming from work he has done during the last five years. He is a very talented author and Mary supported him and supplied him information about Space

Key, so he could dedicate his efforts to writing this book. I would like to submit a copy for evidence." Joe handed a copy to the bailiff who relayed it to the judge.

The judge flipped through a few pages. "Mr. Giovanni, do you think you will get this published?"

Bill started to answer.

Judge O'Day interrupted him. "You stand when you address the court."

Bill stood up. "I don't know, your Honor. It is very difficult to get published, but I may."

The judge continued, "How long have you been working on this?"

Darleen Lynch stood up to object. "Your Honor, I respectively request that you allow me to do the questioning."

"This is my courtroom, Miss Lynch, and I can ask any questions I want." He turned to look at Bill. "I asked you a question! How long have you been working on this book?"

Bill was sweating profusely and kept looking to Darleen for help. Finally, Darleen stood up and asked the judge for a fifteen-minute recess.

That night, Bill and Mary's trial was the leading story on the local news. Fox Network even ran a segment on their national broadcast. The morning talk shows were all discussing if Mary had any rights to Bill's novel. Joe Black made sure there were leaks about the content of *Space Key*. As a result, Joe Black had received over thirty requests for copies of *Space Key* from publishers and agents.

He secretly prepared Bill for the next day's questioning. "Remember, the harder the judge is on you, the better the press coverage will be. I want you to come to court in jeans and a Bad Boy's Bail Bonds t-shirt. I want Judge O'Day and the press to hate you."

Bill was shaking from drinking too much the night before. "I don't know if I can handle this, Joe."

"Don't shave or take a shower. Make a flippant comment. If you get thrown in jail for contempt, we'll keep the publicity going."

The next morning, Bill showed up in court as directed. He even drank a couple of Jamesons for courage. Darleen Lynch looked at Bill when he entered the courtroom. "What the hell are you doing showing up like this?"

Bill answered, "I got drunk last night and woke up just in time to get here." He reeked of stale beer, sweat, and bourbon.

"Do you want to lose this case? I am going to ask for a recess so you can get cleaned up. Don't you dare think about having another drink until this case is over!" Darleen was never given an opportunity to make her request.

When the bailiff announced for all to stand, Bill stayed in his seat. Judge O'Day looked at him. "Mr. Giovanni, please rise."

Bill stood up and said, "What?"

"Bailiff, please put Mr. Giovanni in custody for contempt. I think you need a night in jail; it will give you a little respect for the legal system."

At exactly nine-thirty a.m. the following morning, six black Cadillac Escalades arrived at the Space Key parking lot. Tony Polanski led fifteen FBI agents in black suits into the lobby, each carrying a stack of cardboard file boxes still bound by white shrink wrap. He handed the receptionist, Chrystal, a warrant and flashed his FBI badge. "Lead me to Steven Case's office now and do not call his office first."

Wide eyed, Chrystal froze. Finally, she stood up and said, "I have to call Mr. Case for his permission to let anyone into the offices."

Tony turned to Jack McKee standing next to him and said, "Arrest her for obstruction of a warrant." Jack set down his stack of boxes and pulled out his handcuffs.

"OK," Chrystal said, "follow me."

As the procession started down an aisle of cubicles, Tony said, "Faster."

Chrystal started jogging down the hall until she reached Steven's office. The agents stormed the office and closed the door. After three hours, Jack McKee came out and requested that Chrystal call the stockroom and have them bring four hand trucks to Steven's office. A half-hour later, the agents removed the filled boxes and his computer.

As they were loading the boxes into the back of the Escalades, two news crews were there attempting to get a statement. Marsha Lowe of Channel 9 news asked if Space Key was being investigated for espionage.

Tony Polanski said, "No comment."

Gary Clark was broadcasting live on KGO radio. "Sir, what is the FBI looking for?"

Again, Tony responded, "No comment."

Gary then asked "Does this raid have anything to do with *Space Key,* the novel Bill Giovanni wrote?"

Tony answered, "I cannot comment on an ongoing investigation." He walked away and helped finish loading the boxes.

Gary continued broadcasting, "The FBI is not commenting on the reason for the raid but there is speculation that the contents of Bill Giovanni's novel aren't just fiction. Did executives at Space Key leak classified military projects to the Chinese government? Is Mr. Giovanni's claim true that an executive at Space Key gave the Chinese codes so they could track our submarines? I count fifteen agents loading dozens of boxes into the back of their SUVs." Gary finished with, "Back to you," before he got back into the KGO broadcast truck.

Joe Black was listening to KGO on his way to the Santa Clara County jail where Bill was being held in contempt. He parked his black Mercedes SLK in a reserved space for the assistant prosecutor, who Joe assumed wouldn't be in for an hour.

When he entered the jail, Javari, the clerk behind a desk, said, "Hi, Joe; what are you doing here today?"

Joe gave Javari a big smile. "I am here to see a prisoner, Bill Giovanni."

Javari stared at Joe with a confused expression. He looked at the counter to see that Bill's attorney was Darleen Lynch. Before he could say anything, Joe pulled a small envelope from his inside coat pocket. "I have two box seats to the Giant's game tomorrow night that I can't use. They're playing the Dodgers. Can you use them?"

Javari took the envelope and said, "I will get him."

Joe met with Bill in a prisoner conference room. "If anyone from the police or FBI wants to talk to you, don't say anything without having me there."

Bill was losing his nerve after Joe had told him about the huge raid at Space Key. He hadn't slept at all while he was in the county jail.

Joe said, "You look horrible and they could easily get you to incriminate yourself. Remember, don't agree to talk to them. If you just say you want your lawyer, they will have to stop." Joe pulled out his cell phone. "What's Mary's number? You need to tell her the same. The problem is that I am not your lawyer. Ms. Lynch is. You need to tell Mary not to say anything, then hand the phone to me." He handed Bill the phone.

When Mary answered, she was hysterical. "Do you know what's happening? The FBI raided Space Key. It is all because of this stupid book."

"Calm down, Mary. Joe Black said that we are not to talk to the police or the FBI. If they contact you, demand to talk to your lawyer, Joe."

Bill handed the cell phone to Joe. "Mary, don't worry. I will protect you just don't talk to anyone."

Joe hung up and turned to Bill, "You asshole! You lied to me and now have me involved in an espionage investigation. I will request a continuance for one day due to the new developments. It will give you a chance to clean up and get some sleep. You need to level with me. I can't help you if I don't know everything. I know what our next move will be, but we need to wait until we see what the FBI will do."

"OK," Bill said, "but not here. At your office."

Rodger arrived at work late and missed all the excitement. The workplace was alive with speculation. Everyone was discussing their own theories about why the FBI raided Steve Case's office. He cornered Peggy to fill him in on what happened.

"I can't believe I missed it. I so wanted to see Steven hauled away in handcuffs."

Peggy pushed her hair into shape. "I never believed the accusations you have been making could be true. I thought you were just pissed off because of the way Steven treated you." She tucked her blouse into her skirt. "They didn't arrest Steven," she said. "He's still in his office. Nobody has come or gone since the FBI left."

She looked at the clock and said, "It's one-thirty already. Nobody is going to get any work done today. Do you want to get lunch with me?"

Rodger stood speechless for a minute, "Yeah, sure. Actually, I recently found a great place called Faultline. Are you a beer drinker?"

Tony Polanski was waiting for Bill as he left the county jail. He walked up beside Bill on the sidewalk, pulled out his badge, and said he wanted to ask him some questions. Bill responded, "I will not talk to you without my lawyer present and neither will my wife."

Bill reeked of stale beer and the musty smell from the jail's drunks and homeless. It had been two days since he had taken a shower or slept. Tony pushed Bill face down on the concrete, cuffed him, and said, "You are under arrest for obstruction of a federal investigation. You have the right to an attorney. Are you going to talk to me or do I need to show you the inside of a real jail?"

Bill's nose was bleeding and he couldn't move. "You do what you need to, but I am not talking to you without my lawyer present."

Tony pushed his face into the concrete again. "I can hold you for seventy-two hours."

Bill insisted he be allowed to call Darleen Lynch. His face and wrist throbbed as Tony uncuffed him. Darleen was in Judge O'Day's chambers with the judge, Joe Black, and Mary. Lynch agreed to postpone the trial for one day.

Joe, Darleen, Mary, and Bill were scheduled for a meeting the next morning at ten a.m. in Darleen's office.

Bill wasn't worried about himself at this point. His thoughts were of Mary. Why did I get Mary involved in this? I should have listened to her. Bill was crying. She isn't strong enough; this will break her.

Tony Polanski and Jack McFee were not going to get discouraged by the obstacles created by Bill and

Mary's attorneys. They still had search warrants for any Space Key documentation found at Bill or Mary's residences. They split up, with Tony casing the Hacienda and Jack at Mary's house.

Tony was passing time watching a beautiful girl lying beside the pool in a very small bikini. She would occasionally jump into the pool and swim a lap, then get out and continue sunbathing. When she lay face down, she would untie her top to avoid a tan line. Tony got his binoculars out and watched as the beautiful girl, none other than Irene, sat up to drink her ice tea. He enjoyed a good look at her exposed nipples. I lucked out, he thought. Poor Jack is watching a house and I have my own entertainment.

Bill drove his red El Camino into the motel parking lot and stopped in front of his unit. Tony was surprised to see Irene quickly jump up from the lounge with her top in hand, completely exposing herself. She nonchalantly wrapped her top around her waist to tie the string, twist it around, and pull it up in place. She took a moment to adjust her breasts in the cups. She ran over to the car and leaped on Bill, wrapping her legs and arms around him and kissed him. Tony waited for a couple of minutes until they separated and Bill opened the door. Tony rushed over and shoved his foot in the door jamb, preventing Bill from closing it. He had his FBI badge in one hand and the search warrant in the other. "I have a search warrant. You are welcome to call your attorney but it is valid this time. I am going to search your room."

Irene said to Bill, "What's going on?"

Bill said, "Don't talk to him. He's looking for copies of my novel."

"I don't understand. Why?"

Bill hugged Irene and said, "He thinks Mary and I are involved in espionage at Space Key. I am going to move back in with her because she needs me now."

Bill released his grip on Irene, expecting her to be upset with him.

Irene turned to Tony and said, "Are you really with the FBI?"

Tony said, "Yes. You two stay over there out of my way." He proceeded to open every drawer and dumped the contents onto the bed. Tony found four of the copies that Rodger had made. He searched Bill and took his cell phone. In the closet, he found Irene's belongings and tossed them onto the bed as well. In her backpack, he found the copy of *Space Key* that she had printed off for herself and put it with the other manuscripts.

"Hey," Irene said, "That's mine."

She reached over to grab it and Tony grabbed her hand. "I have a warrant for any items related to Space Key. Don't interfere again." After Tony searched the room, he picked up Irene's manuscript and put it on the hood of the El Camino. He opened the car and examined it for any other evidence. Irene took the opportunity to get out of her wet swimsuit, not caring that the door was open. Tony turned to see her facing him, completely nude. She dried herself with a motel towel and reached up and used the towel to squeeze her hair dry. She took her pink thong off the bed and slipped it on. She pulled up a denim mini skirt and a paisley halter top.

Tony walked back into the room and placed the manuscript back on the bed. "How are you connected with Bill Giovanni?"

Irene stared at Tony's perfect body. "We were dating, but I guess Bill is going back to his wife. I'm not a home wrecker, so I guess I'm not his girlfriend anymore."

Tony didn't object as Irene stepped closer and felt his bicep. Tony said, "Why do you have a copy of his novel?"

"I made a copy for myself when he came to my job at Kinko's to have copies made. It was so good I needed to have one to read for myself." She reached over to the bed and picked up a few pages of the other manuscripts and said, "I didn't print these. Look, these are single spaced and on cheap paper." She showed Tony her copy and said, "See how much better my copy is?"

Tony was interested in the copies as he looked directly at Irene. She dressed in front of me so nonchalantly. She is beautiful. He pulled out his notepad and said, "Write down your address and phone number. I'll need to talk to you later, alone."

He handed the pad and his business card to Irene, who looked up at his blue eyes and said, "OK."

CHAPTER 31

October 17, 1989

Rodger and the entire Bay Area were anticipating game three of the World Series. The Oakland A's won the first two games in Oakland, but now the game moved across the bay to Candlestick Park on the south edge of San Francisco Bay. "The Stick" was infamous for its cold, windy weather, but this was October and Indian summer. The weather for the game was to be unseasonably warm. Rick Reuschel was scheduled to pitch.

Rodger hadn't been much of a baseball fan until this year. All his friends and coworkers talked about was the World Series. Rodger got caught up in the excitement. Tuesday was normally a day that Rodger worked late but today was different. Xing Juan bent over Rodger's computer to see what he was working on. His desk was its normal mess of Post-it[a] notes and half-eaten food. He was focused on writing a difficult code for the Navy stealth submarine. He was unaware of Xing Juan's presence until she said, "If you change the formula using X as the difference of the speed of light times pi it might help."

Rodger looked up. She was holding a folder of paper. Xing Juan's long, jet-black hair hung over her shoulders. Her red blouse hung down, exposing her white, small, firm breasts. Her small body was still even more beautiful at thirty-two than it was when he first met her. His concentration on the formula evaporated. "Let's go to Murphy's Sports Bar in Los Gatos and watch the game," Rodger said.

Xing Juan stood up when she realized where Rodger's focus was. "I thought you wanted to finish this code tonight. Besides, I hate sports!"

Rodger face turned red. "It's not just the game; it's the excitement of being part of the crowd. This is the first time the A's and Giants have ever met in the World Series. I promise you will get a rush just from the energy of the crowd."

Xing Juan crossed her arms, uninterested.

"If you come, I will buy you a double cone at Baskin-Robbins after the game."

Xing Juan smiled. "OK, I'll go. I just don't understand why you stare at my boobs. They're so small."

Rodger turned his red face away and said, "I think they're beautiful."

Xing Juan said, "You liar, but thank you. Also, I can't leave until I fax these twenty pages to New York"

Rodger looked at his watch: it was four p.m. He only had an hour to see the first pitch. He took the pages from her and went to the copy room to fax them for her. While he was gone, Xing Juan took out a high-density floppy disc and inserted it into Rodger's computer to copy the Stealth code. The computer continued to make clicks and spinning sounds. Xing Juan looked in every direction, checking to see if anyone was paying attention to her. After ten minutes, she looked toward the break room. It seemed to take an eternity to make the copy. It finally finished and she saw Rodger walking back just as she ejected the disc.

Los Gatos is a town in an exclusive area, very expensive, located in the hills between San Jose and Santa Cruz. It has a beautiful old downtown full of restaurants and bars. They arrived at the bar a little after four-thirty and it was already packed. Rodger found a small, round pub table with a good view of the TV. Xing Juan sat at the table while Rodger went to order food and drinks. He returned with a beer and hamburger for himself and a crab salad and martini for Xing Juan. They had to shout to hear each other. Customers were all shouting across the bar and room. Most everyone wore a team sweatshirt and cap. Some of them were being ribbed about their silly caps that were split one side green and gold A's and the other side black and orange Giants.

The cross-Bay rivalry was very spirited. The Giants fans outnumbered the A's but the A's had bragging rights. They had won four world titles in the 1970s while the Giants hadn't won since they moved to San Francisco in 1958. Xing Juan and Rodger finished their food and were drinking their second round as game announcer Al Michaels discussed the match-up on the TV.

It was almost impossible to understand with all the bragging each fan was making about their team. The noise increased as the liquor consumption increased. One fan shouted, "Let's go, Giants!" and immediately a group of Oakland fans answered, "Let's go, Oakland!"

By 5:04 p.m., the chant had alternated about six times, until suddenly the building jolted. The TV crashed to the floor. The entire cabinet of bottles behind the bar fell forward onto the customers. Ceiling tiles crashed down on everyone in the bar, creating a choking dust cloud. Xing Juan, thrown from her chair, screamed as she grabbed Rodger, who kept her from falling all the way to the floor and being trampled by the panicked crowd. Rodger picked up Xing Juan's shaking body and charged toward the door along with most of the other customers. He was surprised by how light she was.

Outside, Rodger held Xing Juan, who was in tears, sobbing. He surveyed Los Gatos Boulevard. It resembled a war zone. Not a single storefront window had survived. The bakery next door was completely collapsed to the ground. Bricks were scattered on the street. Rodger stood Xing Juan up and said, "We need to get out of here."

He held her hand as he worked his way through the dazed crowd filling the street. His car was parked on a side street two blocks away. The street had some downed trees and power lines, but Rodger knew the back streets and he lived only a half-mile away. He turned on the radio to KGO, but it was off the air. KGO's broadcast towers had collapsed in the quake. He changed the station to KCBS, and he and Xing Juan listened to the updates of the damage.

The Bay Bridge was closed because a section of the upper deck had collapsed. The double-decker Cypress Freeway in Oakland had collapsed, trapping hundreds of motorists under tons of concrete. The Goodyear blimp had been covering the game and was in position to give visual updates of the devastation. Apartment buildings and homes in the exclusive San Francisco Marina District were destroyed when the landfill they were built on liquefied. Fire broke out and quickly spread. The fire department was frustrated as the water mains had broken and the hydrants had no water. They brought pumps to the bay and volunteers painstakingly helped drag fire hoses to the fires. It took almost two hours before Rodger and Xing Juan made it to his home. All the traffic lights were out. It was now pitch black with no power to light the street lights. It was eerie. Rodger drove these streets every day, but in this darkness he was lost and confused.

They arrived at Rodger's home in Campbell about seven-thirty. The darkness made it difficult to find their way to the front door. Rodger tried to unlock the dead bolt but needed both hands to turn the key. When it finally clicked open, he needed to push the door with his shoulder as the jamb had shifted. He had Xing Juan wait at the door while he felt his way into the kitchen where he kept a flashlight in a drawer. When he turned on the flashlight, he could see dishes broken on the kitchen floor. The living room lamp was lying on its side, broken. His fifty-gallon aquarium was still on its stand but a foot of water was gone. The hardwood floor was soaked and two angel fish and six mollies lay dead on the floor. Rodger cleaned up the water with a couple of large bath towels. He and Xing Juan sat on the couch.

"I have never been in an earthquake before," she said. "I am still shaking. I have never been so frightened in my life."

Rodger held her tight. His heart was beating hard as he felt her body pressed against his. He leaned back to see Xing Juan's lily white face, gently put his fore-finger under her chin to pull her face closer to his, and kissed her.

Xing Juan started to pull away but suddenly felt the comfort of being embraced. She stopped shaking, relaxed, and reached her hands around the back of Rodger's head to continue the kiss. She wrapped her arms around him. Rodger ran his arms up and down her back. Xing Juan continued to kiss him. The next pass of his hands up her back was underneath her loose blouse. He reached his hands around and caressed her breasts. He lifted the blouse over her head and off.

As he started to unhook her bra, Xing Juan said, "No, they're so small. I don't want you to see them."

Rodger continued to unfasten the bra. He looked at her bare chest. "Xing Juan, you are beautiful." He bent over to suck her nipples and they quickly became erect. They made love, unaware of the constant sounds of sirens. They talked throughout the night. Xing Juan told Rodger how her brother was under house arrest for his involvement in Falun Gong.

The next morning, they woke to see the mess the house was in. There was still no power. The only news came from Bill's portable radio. The epicenter was south of Santa Cruz in Aptos, just thirty miles from them. The historic Old Downtown of Santa Cruz had been built of brick. Every building collapsed instantly when the quake hit. Rescue efforts were under way trying to dig out any survivors. In the East Bay, rescue workers risked their lives crawling between the collapsed layers of the freeway, not knowing if an aftershock might crush them as well. The World Series was credited for saving lives as it happened at rush hour. Normally, the Cypress Freeway would have been jammed, but not that night, as people left work early to see the game.

Xing Juan was still frightened. She held Rodger as he surveyed the rubble in his own home. He led her back to the bedroom where they made love again. Rodger felt passion surging through his body. Even with all the damage, he was content just to have Xing Juan sleeping through the night with him. He pulled her naked body upright so they faced each other. He kissed her and then said, "I love you. Will you marry me?"

Xing Juan pulled away, feeling shock that Rodger was serious. "Rodger, I love you too, but you are my best friend. I can't marry you. Besides, I am in love with Steven."

Rodger couldn't believe what he heard. "Are you talking about Steven Case?"

She nodded her head.

"He's married!" Rodger paused, not knowing what to say. "Are you sleeping with him?"

Tears rolled down Xing Juan's face. "Yes, but only a few times. We were on business trips and it just happened. It was when I first started with Space Key and he encouraged me so much."

"He's married, Xing Juan!" Rodger said emphatically.

"I know, but he's not happy and he said he would leave his wife even if he had not met me." Xing Juan pulled the sheet up to cover her body.

"How long ago did he tell you he would leave his wife?" Rodger asked.

Xing Juan was sobbing uncontrollably, "About four years ago when we were at the electronics convention together."

"Can't you see that he's using you? He will never leave his wife." Rodger was frustrated. "Do you know who she is? She's Samantha Key; her grandfather started Space Key and her family are the major stockholders. That is the only reason he has his position there."

Rodger got up, put on some clothes, and began picking up the mess in silence. At noon, he drove Xing Juan back to her car at Space Key. They went in to see if the building was operational. The building seemed to be standing, but all the suspended ceiling tiles had fallen down, covering every desk, file cabinet, and office machine in the building with a thick, gray dust. It was apparent that Space Key would be closed for some time.

CHAPTER 32

September 7, 2000

Bill and Mary had an appointment with Joe Black and Darleen Lynch at Darleen's office. Mary was silent, staring straight ahead, chewing on her thumbnail. Already the sidewalk was crowded with office workers, attorneys, and plaintiffs off to court. Bill walked around and opened the door for Mary. She abruptly pushed him away and stepped out. Her right arm tremored and Bill could see she was on the verge of an anxiety attack. She marched down the street without waiting while Bill locked the truck.

"I know I screwed up but we need to talk before we see the attorneys."

"There's a coffee shop right here. We have a half hour to kill."

He rushed ahead and opened the door, hoping Mary would follow. She stopped and looked at Bill holding the door.

"Fucker," she said as she turned to enter the building. She spotted four men in suits running toward them. Quickly, they slammed the door closed.

Tony Polanski pulled out his FBI badge and an envelope. "Mary Giovanni!"

The two other men held Bill back. "You can't do this!" yelled Bill. One agent shoved him to the ground, pressing his face into the pavement.

Tony and his partner Tom spun Mary around and crammed her into the glass door. The metal frame of the door painfully pressed into her face and chest. Tony pulled his handcuffs out, but Mary's right arm flung above her head. Tom grabbed her wrist and yanked it down so Tony could cuff her. "You are under arrest for espionage and releasing classified military information."

Darleen Lynch's office was busy with interns making copies and the receptionist fielding nonstop phone calls. Darleen and Joe heard the commotion and rushed into the waiting room.

Bill ran into the office, panting, "Where is Joe Black?" Bill supported himself with his hand on the reception counter to catch his breath. "Mary was just arrested by the FBI in front of your office!"

★★★

The Robert F. Peckham Federal Building on First Street in San Jose was an imposing, old, outdated brick building. Tony Polanski, District Attorney Carlos Marquez, and Steven Case sat around a steel desk in a glass-partitioned office with fluorescent lighting. Carlos looked at Steven.

"Thank you for your assistance for the last two years in our investigation into spying. Tony confiscated four copies of the novel *Space Key*. However, he discovered one copy that is an original. There had been editing on the recent version which tried to implicate you in the espionage case. We suspect the same individual planted the evidence on your computer and in your office."

"That's impossible," Steven said, "I always keep my office locked. How could anyone doctor my computer?"

"I marked the pages that have the character "Alex." Read them and tell us if you recognize any of your employees that could be him as we think he is the one leaking information."

Steven spent fifteen minutes reading the marked pages. "That is Rodger Hinds. He has been with Space Key for twenty-five years. He has been a pain in the ass for a long time now but I can't believe he would betray his country." He kept reading, "Fuck! That asshole is accusing me of having an affair with Xing Juan. My wife will divorce me in a heartbeat if this is ever published." He set the book down. "Why do you think he is a suspect?"

"He was a suspect," Tony said, "because we found his phone number on Bill Giovanni's cell phone. Did he have access to your refrigerator?"

"Yeah," Steven said. "I had him in my office often and he always helped himself to a bottle of water. Why does that matter?"

"We have been analyzing everything we took from your office. Today the lab said someone has been putting deionized water into your water bottles. Drinking it even for a short time could kill you."

Steven flipped the manuscript back to Tony. "That explains why I have been so sick. Fucking asshole! Arrest that bastard."

Carlos said, "I would like to get more evidence. We don't need to get a warrant to search his desk with your permission."

Steven said, "Can I come with you?"

Forty-five minutes later, Carlos Marquez, Tony Polanski, Jack McFee, Steven Case, and six additional FBI agents arrived at Space Key. Steven marched them through the building to Rodger Hind's cubicle.

Rodger had just come out of the break room and he watched as they searched his desk. Tony pulled open the bottom file drawer of his desk and carefully removed six water bottles that were the same type found in Steven's refrigerator.

Steven repeated, "That asshole."

Tony picked up a ring of keys out of the drawer. "I bet one of these keys will open Mr. Case's office."

Rodger had seen enough and turned toward the exit. Shit, they aren't arresting Steven, he surmised. That fucker Bill double-crossed me. I should have never trusted him after he got me drunk. Now he turned me in. Paybacks are a bitch. Shit! Rodger made it to the parking lot without being noticed.

Felix, the IT expert for Space Key, sat down at Rodger's computer and opened a CD. It was a copy of *Space Key*. He then started searching programs. When he found the software code for the stealth submarine project, he tried to open it but it was password locked. Steven said, "Let me unlock it," and quickly punched in his administrator password.

Felix now had access to everything in the computer. He opened the source files, which covered the screen with X's and O's. "This file has been regularly copied to a disc on a weekly basis for almost ten years until eighteen months ago," Felix said. "Was there an event that happened on that date?"

Steven said, "That's when Xing Juan left for Hong Kong to visit her family."

"Xing Juan, in the novel?"

"Yes. Her name is Xing Juan Kang. She was a brilliant scientist, and she started working here when she was only nineteen. She already had a PhD from MIT. She worked with me very closely and became a good friend. However, she was not very stable. She was murdered at the Peninsula Hotel in Hong Kong eighteen months ago. I can't believe she was the leak! I trusted her. You can't let them publish this book."

"Don't worry, Steven; we will claim that all the material is classified information."

CHAPTER 33

Joe Black arrived at the questioning room at the county jail. It was a small room with faded gray-painted walls. There were two secured doors at each end of the room. Mary's right hand was handcuffed to a small, square steel table in the center of the room. Tears were dropping onto her orange jumpsuit with the large black letters SCCJ both on the front and back. A tape recorder was on the table.

Tony Polanski said, "Mrs. Giovanni, I have everything I need to convict you, so just tell me everything and I will go easy on you."

"Bullshit!" Joe threw his business card on the table in front of Tony. "I am Joe Black, Mary Giovanni's attorney, and anything you may have badgered out of her you can't use. Get the fuck out of here and let me talk to my client."

Tony stood up. "I'm just questioning a dangerous suspect. She has compromised the security of our military."

"Did you read Mary her Miranda rights"

Tony didn't answer.

"Yooz cops are always trying to bully your way through. You are full of shit! We both know that Mary Giovanni never had access to classified information. Now get the fuck out of here so I can meet with my client."

"I just doing my job. Mary's a suspect." Tony took a long pause. "OK, I will give you ten minutes."

"I will take as long as I want, and I'm dead ass serious."

Tony, without saying anything, started to leave the room. Joe grabbed Tony's sleeve. "Uncuff her, please. Mary isn't going anywhere."

Tony complied and used his key to unlock the handcuff on Mary's wrist and then left the room.

Mary sprang up and hugged Joe. "Thank you for coming."

Joe patted her back, gave her a hug, and guided her to her chair. "Mary, you're too tight. Just sit still and breathe."

Mary was soaked in sweat and trembling. He held her hands clasped between his.

"Did you tell them anything?"

Mary took a few deep breaths. "I couldn't speak. I was so scared."

"OK, Mary. You did the right thing. You are leaving here today with me. I promise."

Joe pulled the chair Tony had across the table and moved it to sit next to Mary. He put his arm on her shoulder. "They aren't allowed to record anything we talk about but I don't trust them. I going to whisper and you just nod yes or no."

Mary nodded her head yes. She had already stopped shaking.

Joe whispered in her ear, "Do you know how classified information got into the book?"

Mary shook her head no.

Joe continued to whisper his questions: "Bill doesn't work at Space Key, so do you know who helped him?"

Mary held her palms up and whispered, "Maybe. Bill was worried about someone who could wreck his plan."

Joe asked Mary more questions and realized that she didn't have anything to do with the book. He gave Mary another hug. "We're tight. I'm going to talk to Tony and get you out of here now."

Joe left the room and met with Tony. "Let's go outside so I can have a cigarette."

They walked through the booking room toward the front door. The room was loud with cops, attorneys, and suspects all trying to talk over each other.

Joe pulled a pack out of his shirt pocket and tapped the bottom to get a few cigarettes to pop up. He turned the pack to Tony. Tony took one out, as did Joe. He pulled a Zippo lighter out and lit both cigarettes. They paused for a couple of minutes while they enjoyed their smokes. Finally, Joe said, "You have shit against Mary and you know it. This is just harassment. She just worked on the assembly line and had no access to classified information. She has a young child at home and isn't going anywhere."

They both continued smoking.

"I want you to release her to me. I will make sure she stays available."

Tony lifted his finger as if to make a comment but stopped what he intended to say. "OK, you have a point, but I want her to sign a statement that she will not leave the county. We can all meet tomorrow."

Tony put his hand out to shake. Joe grabbed his hand and took a step forward and gave him an embrace.

Joe waited until Mary was allowed to dress back into her clothes and then he drove her back to his office. Mary had calmed down and was able to speak. "Thank you. I was so scared I just fell apart."

"You did great." Joe gave Mary another hug. "You don't need to worry. I will take care of this."

Other than Bill, this was the first time that Mary didn't panic when a man touched her. She felt safe with this outrageous, tough New Yorker and found she could talk without the usual feelings of uneasiness. Joe picked up his phone and called Darleen Lynch's office. He set a meeting for tomorrow at two in the afternoon for Darleen, Bill, Mary, and Joe to meet at Darleen's office with Tony Polanski joining at two-thirty.

CHAPTER 34

It was a warm afternoon in downtown San Jose. Darleen Lynch's office was paneled in reddish rich mahogany. She sat at the head of a long conference table. It had oak strips of different hues much like a hardwood floor. Under the table were plugs to accommodate anyone's laptop computer. Darleen's lips were tightly closed while she tapped her pencil on the desk. Bill sat next to her on her left side. Joe Black wore his black leather jacket, a crimson red shirt with silver buttons, and a black fedora. He sat on the right side with Mary next to him biting her fingernails. Betty and an assistant came in with coffee, cream, and sugar. She gave everyone a cup and set the tray in the middle of the table.

Darleen said, "Please close the door when you leave."

As soon as the door was closed, she stared at Joe. "You bastard! You set me up. I run a simple divorce practice and now I have the FBI coming in to question our clients and we could be involved with an espionage ring."

Joe reached out his arms, interlocked his fingers, and stretched. "Oh, darling, shit happens sometimes."

Before he could finish, she said, "Don't you ever call me darling. It is Ms. Lynch to you!"

"Oh my," Joe said, "yooz a bit testy."

"I am fuckin' pissed off and if I can get you disbarred, I will!" Darleen stood up and walked around the table with her pencil, slapping it on her palm. "We need to make a plan before the FBI arrive. I don't want to be disbarred or have my practice become implicated in an espionage plot."

Bill and Mary sat silently as the two attorneys bickered with each other.

Darleen said, "Bill, can you tell me what is really going on?"

"I'm not sure, Ms. Lynch. I'm just a bartender who has Space Key regulars that come into the bar. I've been listening to their gossip since I was a teenager and wrote their stories down."

Darleen snapped her pencil. "You're not smart enough to write a grocery list, let alone this novel. If you keep giving me this bullshit, I am going to excuse myself from your case. I will not be made a patsy." She looked across the table at Joe. "You asshole, you know what's going on and I'll bet you sent Bill to me just for the publicity factor."

"Calm down, Ms. Lynch," Joe said, as he pulled a cigar out of his breast pocket. "I am merely representing Mary in this divorce case. I have no knowledge of any illegal activities. I suggest we deal with the immediate problem of what we will do when the FBI agents arrive."

Darleen was furious but she needed to be pragmatic right now, as she'd had little time to prepare her client, Bill. "Bill, who gave you the classified information in the book?"

Bill looked at Joe first.

"Fuck you, Bill, as well!" Darleen said. "I am your attorney; you answer to me. I knew you and Joe had concocted this sham and pulled me into it thinking I would be a dumb dupe."

Bill looked at Darleen. "I just gathered the information from gossip at the bar. It was my Uncle John's bar and I have been around the bar since I was thirteen. I can't remember everyone who told stories about Space Key.

Betty knocked on the door and opened it.

Tony and Jack pushed their way past Betty and nodded at the group. "Betty, Jack and I would love a cup of coffee as well, mine black and cream in Jack's."

Tony sat beside Mary and Jack next to Bill. "Who has any other copies of this book?" Tony asked Mary.

Mary looked puzzled. "I don't know what you are talking about. Bill wrote the book."

Tony said, "We want every copy so this information can't be released to the public."

Joe interrupted. "If you have any questions, you need to ask me first. I am her counsel and she doesn't have to talk to you."

Tony looked at Joe and said, "This is an espionage case and Mary needs to cooperate or we will arrest her again right now."

Mary shook and stuttered, "I d–don't understand."

Tony continued, "We have three years of e-mails between you and Steven Case discussing meetings and classified information on CDs that came from you. You worked at Space Key so the information could have only come from you."

Mary looked at Bill with tears rolling down her face. Bill sat there, stunned.

Tony placed a subpoena on the table for all copies of the novel. "If you don't turn over every copy now, I will have everyone in this room arrested for obstruction of a federal investigation and conspiracy to commit espionage."

Darleen and Joe huddled together at the back of the room, trying not to be heard by Tony and Jack. Darleen said "fuck" to Joe repeatedly. "You fucker, you got me into this just to help Bill." She waved her hands and pointed her finger into Joe's face.

Joe hadn't moved for about five minutes while Darleen vented. "I didn't think any of this would happen. You have to forget about it and deal with what we have now. Let me handle this."

They came back to the table. Joe said to Tony, "We will give you the one copy we have so you can see what's in the novel. However, this is the property of Bill and it will be published!"

"I have an order for all copies," Tony said as he pushed the paper toward Joe. "We have determined that the entire book contains classified information."

"Well, we don't have any other copies. I think you've already collected the rest of them. I will be in court shortly, challenging your subpoena."

"I want to know who your source is!" Tony demanded. "The FBI isn't interested in you and if you cooperate, I may be able to cut you a deal."

Joe stood up, grabbed the subpoena, and said, "This meeting is over. Please leave! We can pick it up Monday after we have more time to talk to our clients.

Tony Polanski and Jack McFee left with the one manuscript. Darleen looked at Joe and said, "What the fuck is going on?"

Joe looked at Bill and said, "We have to level with Darleen now that this is becoming a criminal case." He redirected his focus to Darleen. "Will you agree to be co-counsel with me on any criminal case against Mary or Bill? Otherwise, I can't discuss this with you."

Darleen thought for a while. "I'm not qualified to do this. I've been a divorce attorney for twenty years."

"Darleen, don't underestimate yourself," Joe said. "I sent Bill to you because I know you are ruthless and not afraid of a courtroom battle. Besides, I will be the lead and I don't think they got squat to work with."

"OK, but I am still pissed off at you." Darleen slammed her hands on the desk in front of Bill. "Can you tell me what is going on?"

Bill was anxious. "Mary and I don't want a divorce. I went to Joe Black because I thought I could get publicity to sell my novel by having the novel become the focus of our divorce. And it worked! But I had no idea it would lead to this."

Darleen started to pace across the front of the room. Her high heels clicked with each step. "How did you get classified information in the book and why is Mary having meetings with Steven Case?"

"A lot of Space Key employees hang out at Kelly's Bar. I've known them since I was thirteen. John Kelly was my uncle and like a father to me. They get drunk and talk a lot. And I don't know about Steven Case."

Mary stuttered, "I never met Steven Case. And I don't have his e-mail address."

Joe Black butted in. "If that is true, and I believe you, then there is someone on the inside setting you up. You haven't told us the whole story." He looked at Bill. "Who helped you with this? There is too much technical information for you to have written this without help."

Mary looked at Bill, glad that Darleen had stopped asking her questions. She thought why did I tell Bill about the novel on the computer?

Bill said, "I do have one source that helped me but I promised not to involve him. Can't a writer keep his sources confidential?"

"Bill," Joe said firmly, "We're your attorneys; what you tell us is protected. Neither Ms. Lynch nor I can give any information to anyone that you tell us. That is why I asked her to be co-counsel for any criminal case. If you can't level with us, find yourself another attorney!"

Bill thought for a moment. "If I give you his name, can you promise not to talk to him? He won't answer any of your questions anyway."

Joe interrupted Darleen's pacing and took her to the side. "Bill is probably right that he won't talk to us, but I could have my private investigator check him out. I think we should agree not to talk to him."

"OK, Bill. Ms. Lynch and I will not talk to him if you tell us who he is and what information he gave you."

Bill said, "Rodger Hinds. He is a computer nerd at Space Key and he hates the place. He supplied all the technical information in the book. I didn't realize he was giving me classified information, just technical stuff to make the novel more interesting, He asked for all the copies and the disc so he could remove himself from the story. He rewrote it without him in it. That is why we asked for your copies back so Rodger could revise them."

"Fuck!" Joe said. "Rodger has us over a barrel with all the original copies."

Bill interrupted, "I still have the original novel on a disc that I didn't give to Rodger." He couldn't tell them about the computer or they would have proof that he didn't write the novel.

The meeting in Darleen's office lasted another hour. Bill told Mary there was no reason to continue the divorce, so he would pick up his stuff at the Hacienda Motel and meet her back at the house.

★★★

That Monday, Joe and Darleen prepared Bill and Mary for the questions from the FBI. "Don't answer any question without looking at me first." Joe blinked. "If I do that, you can answer; if not, look at me and I will come up with an answer."

Tony and Jack arrived ten minutes early. "We have e-mails between Mary and Steven Case that confirm her part in this conspiracy. It won't take a jury long to convict." Tony looked at Mary. "Do you have any idea how long twenty-five years in prison is?"

Mary was in a full panic attack, her right arm trembling out of control. She was incapable of talking as tears rolled down her cheek. Her face became expressionless as she stared at the wall.

Bill looked at Joe Black, hoping he would make this end. Joe stood up, holding an unlit cigar between his ring and index finger. "You got nothing, Tony. If you don't release both of them now, I will file a harassment suit against you, the Justice Department, and the Attorney General. Bill is a journalist just doing his job. He has a right to publish his book and will do so."

Tony said, "The copies we found in his car were all altered to destroy evidence."

"We have Bill directly connected to Rodger Hinds," Tony said. "There was a stack of the manuscripts he edited to implicate Steven Case in his desk. Fortunately, Bill's girlfriend Irene saved an original copy, which reveals Rodger as the agent giving Xing Juan top secret information. She was selling it to the Chinese."

Suddenly, Mary snapped out of her panic attack and slapped Bill's face, "Bill's girlfriend Irene! Who the fuck is Irene, Bill? Or should I ask, how long have you been fucking Irene?" She slapped his face again.

Darleen grabbed her and said, "Not now. Not in front of Agent Polanski."

Tony stared into Mary's face. "I will let you walk scot free if you want to testify against Bill. You could leave today"

Joe Black had listened patiently. "If these supposed e-mails were between Mary and Steven Case, why isn't he in this room being charged as well?"

"Mr. Case has agreed to cooperate with the investigation. We will not be filing charges against him," Tony said.

"How long ago did Mr. Case decide to cooperate?"

"That is irrelevant; he has provided us with all the information we need for this prosecution."

"Bullshit! You are leaving this room now unless you charge Bill and Mary or you can tell me when Mr. Case started to cooperate. I will be able to find out by tomorrow with a discovery request."

Sweat shone on Tony's forehead.

Darleen sat back to watch Joe work Tony over, impressed with his ability. "We've leaving now. Bill,

Mary, let's go. They don't have anything to arrest you on."

Tony relented. "OK, Steven Case was never a suspect. He contacted us over two years ago because he suspected someone was selling the Navy's stealth submarine technology to the Chinese. However, he has given us all the evidence we need to prosecute your clients."

"That doesn't make sense," Joe said. "Steven Case would have turned over any e-mails between him and Mary to you long ago. This is all a fabrication to make you look good in catching a spy ring. I am sure you are already working on the press release. Here is the deal I will make you: Bill will agree to remove any formulas from his book in exchange for us not pressing charges for false arrest, tampering with evidence, and harassment." He paused to allow Tony to consider his options, held out his hand and said, "Agreed?"

Tony looked like a beaten dog with his tail between his legs. He reached out and said, "OK."

Joe walked to the door and announced to the room: "Let's go."

Bill walked out first and turned to look at Mary, whose only words were, "You asshole."

As Darleen passed through the door, Joe put his hand on her shoulder and said, "How about a drink to celebrate our victory? I think we make a great team."

Darleen looked into his blue eyes and said, "Fuck you, asshole."

She said to Bill and Mary, "Here is a card of a marriage therapist I greatly admire. You should meet with her before you do something you may regret the rest of your life. You two have a son who needs you and you can work this out."

Mary turned to Joe. "Finish this divorce. Bill put me through hell and he would do it again. Bill can keep his house and bar but I want the rights to the book. Just ask Bill to write a simple paragraph and you will know I wrote it, not him."

Joe looked at Mary. "Let's have dinner tonight." Then he looked at Bill.

"She will win."

Bill said, "Mary, I love you. I will do anything to make it right." Tears were rolling down his face as he tried to give her a hug.

Mary pushed him away. "Don't ever touch me again." She looked at Joe and said, "I know a good Italian restaurant."

"Fuck," Bill said to Joe, "I came to you and now you are taking my wife out."

Joe looked at Bill. "You fucked up your life all on your own."

That evening, Joe wore a long, black suede jacket, a white dress shirt with gold cufflinks, a cream vest, and bright red bow tie. He picked up Mary, who was wearing her new, bright green spring dress, and drove to Palo Alto to have dinner at Joe's favorite restaurant, Li Fornaio.

Mary said, "I'll have the spaghetti," as she sipped red wine.

Joe laughed. "How did I know that is what you would order?"

He told the waiter, "A New York steak and burn the crust."

"Look who's laughing. Tough New Yorker. What else would you order but a burnt steak?"

"The steak isn't burnt. I just want them to make sure the outside is burnt. Adds flavor. You wait and I will give you a piece."

They talked over dinner for two hours.

"I'm having a good time, Joe."

Joe grabbed Mary's hand. "We don't need the evening to end now. Let's go dancing at Alberto's."

Mary, startled, said, "I've never gone dancing. I don't know."

Joe was now holding both of Mary's hands. "It's a salsa club. You will love it. You get to do a lot of spinning. Let's go."

The song "Margarita" blasted as they walked through the doors. Mary stood still as she watched the dancers fast-paced spins and complicated turns with their hands always together. She turned to Joe.

"I can't do that!"

"Sure you can. You don't need to be great to have fun. Besides, you will get the hang of it quickly."

Joe walked Mary through the basic steps and spun her around with their hands above Mary's head.

"You were right; I am having fun." Mary lifted Joe's hand again so he could lead her through another spin.

The band played "Valerie." Joe embraced Mary for the upbeat lyrics while everyone was dancing with their bodies sensually embracing each other. Joe held her with his arms around her back and then kissed her. Mary leaned into him and continued the kiss.

She pulled away and said, "I've never kissed anyone except Bill. I can't believe I can kiss you and feel calm and wonderful."

★★★

Two weeks later, Joe negotiated a one hundred thousand dollar advance for Mary from publisher Random House for the rights to the nonfiction novel, with the understanding that Mary be allowed enough time to add the recent events into the book. "You had a good novel but now that we know the rest of the story, you can change this to a nonfiction nail biter."

Mary laughed and said, "Nobody would know how to write a nail biter better than me."

Mary included Samantha Key's firing and divorce of Steven Case once she found out about the affair; Rodger was arrested and put in a psychiatric hospital, being found unfit to stand trial.

Mary sat at the laptop working to finish the novel as she thought, I can't believe I no longer have to work for that asshole Edmond and put up with his sweaty hands. I never thought life would end up being this good. Joe has given me and Johnny a new life.

ADDENDUM

Diane Feinstein became mayor of San Francisco and continued a long political career. She is currently the senior U.S. senator for California. Jackie Speier survived from the attack at Jonestown and was elected and is currently U.S. House representative for San Mateo County, the seat Leo Ryan held.

Photo credits:

- *USS Macon* at Moffett Field: By NASA Ames Research Center (NASA-ARC) - & Wikipedia: https://www.google.com/search?channel=tus&q=USS+Macon&tbm=isch&source=univ&client=-firefox-b-1-d&sa=X&ved=2ahUKEw-ji3Z_Qst3jAhWmiFQKHTBjDkYQ iR56BAgEEBA&biw=1139&bih=6 19#imgrc=mwHg7u-STkjbNM:
- 1975 AMC Gremlin with Levi's uphol-stery; Wikipedia: https://commons.

wikimedia.org/wiki/File:1974_AMC_
Gremlin_with_Levi%E2%80%99s_
option_at_2015_AMO_show_1of5.jpg

- 1989 A's/Giants baseball cap; eBay: https://
www.ebay.com/itm/Vintage-1989-World-
Series-Battle-Of-The-Bay-Giants-vs-A-s-
Snapback-Cap-Hat/383052592426?hash=i
tem592fb6b52a:g:U3MAAOSwzjNdLV2c